A Gift of Sky

A Gift of Sky

Linda Ghan

Western Producer Prairie Books
Saskatoon, Saskatchewan

Cover painting, "Island in a Timestream," by Douglas Thiell
Cover design by Warren Clark/GDL
Edited by Lois Simmie

The publisher wishes to acknowledge the support received for
this publication from the Canada Council. The author wishes to
thank the Canada Council for an Explorations Grant to research
the book.

Printed and bound in Canada

Western Producer Prairie Books is a unique publishing venture
located in the middle of western Canada and owned by a group
of prairie farmers who are members of Saskatchewan Wheat
Pool. From the first book in 1954, a reprint of a serial originally
carried in the weekly newspaper *The Western Producer,* to the
book before you now, the tradition of providing enjoyable and
informative reading for all Canadians is continued.

Canadian Cataloguing in Publication Data

Ghan, Linda

   A gift of sky

   ISBN 0-88833-254-8

I. Title.

PS8563.H35G5 1988   C813'.54   C88-098086-9
PR9199.3.G42G5 1988

To Sidney Ghan
  who gave me laughter

To Esther Ghan
  who gave me story

Contents

1. THE GARDEN   1

2. BLACKBIRDS   6

3. SUNSETS   13

4. BETH   22

5. LITTLE GIRLS   34

6. GROWING PAINS   49

7. JEWISH GIRLS   64

8. LET ME CALL YOU SWEETHEART   85

9. SCHOOLTEACHERS   103

10. FLOWERS IN THE SKY   120

11. A DIFFERENCE TO THE HORIZON   132

1

The Garden

In the beginning, life was something that happened to you. Like when Mama picked you up and carried you out to see the calf just born and lying sleepy beside its mother. Or when you put your hand out so you wouldn't fall, and there was your hand-print on the door Papa just painted, and Papa was frowning. Or when all of a sudden, it was dark, and you had to come in.

Mama happened, too, with her singing and laughing—blue eyes snapping with laughter or snapping with anger, and long, long black hair with red lights in it. I think I got my temper from her. Papa had black hair, but with blue lights rather than red, and thoughtful, warm, brown-gold eyes. He always smiled first in his eyes. Uncle Yacov had Papa's black hair and the same brown-gold eyes, but they were more laughing eyes. He was a more laughing man. Aunt Sophie, raven black hair and red cheeks, was electrical storms and summer sun. Zaida was my pillow, a big warm pillow with a long white beard and liquid black eyes. He was my pillow who loved me back no matter what.

My earliest memory was me trying to happen to life. Uncle Yacov had picked me up and thrown me into the air so that everything disappeared but me being thrown into the air and him laughing, catching me. Now he wanted to go away. I hid his hat under the bed. They looked and looked for that hat. But he still went away.

The summer I was four, the summer when it hailed and the cat died, I began to notice that even big people could have life happen to them. The nice safe box that frames your life is shattered then, and there aren't any rules after that.

It was hot. So hot that it seemed like the sun had eaten up the blue and filled the sky, and everything in the yard was trying to hide from it. Then, suddenly, the sun was being eaten up by deep black clouds, and Zaida and I were shooing the chickens and turkeys and ducks and geese into the barn, and Mama was standing at the doorway with her arms full of pillows looking out over the fields, at the wheat shimmering green against a wet-black sky. "Look at it," she said. "So beautiful. And so deadly."

We each went off with a pillow to hold against a window so the glass wouldn't break.

And the ice diamonds smashed out of the sky.

Like laughter after tears, the sky cleared to a crystal blue, a meadowlark was singing its clear water-song . . . and all of that shimmering wheat that had been standing up to the sun only minutes before as if to say, "I'm here. I'm beautiful," was now beaten flat against the ground. Mama stood at the door saying over and over, "Oh, no. Oh, no," and "Where's Aaron?"

Papa came in then. He sat down beside the table. He sat down as if he would never get up again. And he put down his head and cried.

The sun was pouring with sleepy warm magic. You couldn't go through the door when the sun was like that, or you'd get caught and be warm and sleepy like the sun. Like the cat was, curled up and warm and furry in the middle of the sunbeam. I poked my arm into the warm sunbeam from the cool shade and stroked the cat's sun-warm fur. He got up and stretched and padded out of the sunbeam to his dish. Then he was back in the sunbeam again, washing his face and smiling.

All of a sudden, like in a bad dream, he changed, no longer smiling, but writhing and yowling. Then—nothing. He lay there. Still. In the sunbeam.

2

Saul crawled in. He pulled himself up on the churn and pulled out the cork and was laughing and splashing in the white cream, a white cream baby. Mama looked at Saul, laughing and splashing, and she looked at the cat lying still, and she picked Saul the white cream baby up and hugged him and kissed him. And she was crying.

Then I was crying and couldn't stop. I didn't know why I was crying, except that something had happened to the smiling part of the cat.

"Come, *medele*." A warm hand closed over mine.

We were in the garden, and Zaida was scooping out a hole with his hands. The cat was just lying there, no longer a cat.

"Where," I asked between sobs, "did it go?"

"What?"

"The smiling part of the cat. Where did it go?"

"I'm going to tell you a story."

He pulled out a radish and a carrot and a potato, a cucumber and a pea pod. He took out his knife and carved little eyes and little noses and little mouths, and then there was a comfortable Mr. Potato with a tummy like Zaida's, and nervous Mrs. Carrot, and young Mr. Pea who was always where he shouldn't be, and Mr. Cucumber who was busy and didn't see Young Pea and rolled right on top of him and snapped him in two.

Mrs. Carrot and Miss Radish were crying, while Mr. Cucumber was just beside himself with grief. But Mr. Potato said, in a voice just like Zaida's, "Life is a story. Just like the garden. There is a beginning, and a middle, and an end. In the beginning, *mein kind*,"—he popped out one of the peas from Young Pea and snuggled it into the earth—"we are all seeds in the spring. At the end of the summer, please God we should live so long, we have white hair, we don't see so good . . . just like your Zaida whose knee you are sitting on.

"But in every story there is good and there is bad. The good—the rain, the sun, Mama and Papa taking care of you— helps you grow. And the bad things . . . from the bad things, you learn what you can do. Because you must struggle. Sometimes, though, the bad things are too strong. Then you go. Like the cat."

"Am I like the cat?" I asked.

3

"No. You and Saul, you have your heads just high enough to see the sun. For you, it is spring."

"Are Mama and Papa and Uncle Yacov and Aunt Sophie at the end of summer?"

"No. They still have things to do."

"Everybody," I decided, "has things to do."

"No." He shook his head. "I am old. I need a cane. What can I do?"

"You take care of me. And the ducks and the chickens."

"Ah. But soon you will take care of yourself and the ducks and the chickens, too."

Sometimes, after the hail and after the cat died, there were fights. It was Zaida and Papa. I didn't know what the fights were about then. I just knew that when big people fought, it was deep black clouds banging into each other, and thunder, and the whole world becoming dark.

The thunder stopped when Papa slammed out of the house. Mama would whisper in my ear, "Take your Zaida for a walk," and I would hold Zaida's hand while he walked along muttering, "No *yamelka*. No beard. My own son. On the Sabbath he harvests. What kind of Jew?"

Suddenly, the muttering would stop. Zaida might be bending down pointing with his cane. "Look. Such a tiny bit of life," and it might be a duckling, still wet and bedraggled and surrounded by fragments of white shell. "So late in the summer. How can this be?" And another, drying out to become a little ball of yellow fluff with little duck feet and a little duck beak.

"Look," he would point again, and a hen might be settling her chicks down for a nap, waiting patiently, wings outstretched, while they scampered up her back, scrambled onto her head, finally nestling under fluffed-out wing and breast feathers so that only tiny toothpick legs were visible.

Of course, like in Zaida's garden, there was bad in the story. It was the gander. The gander hated us. While the chickens and turkeys would continue pecking around our feet, and the ducks and geese waddled away to circle in behind us, the gander always stopped action and took notice with superb irritation, head cocked, wings at the ready, gabbling complaints and orders. One day, he just couldn't stand it. Wings out-stretched, hissing, he came straight at us.

Zaida froze.

And, suddenly, with no recollection of how it had happened, I was between Zaida and the gander with a stick in my hand. The gander had stopped dead in his tracks. We were nose to nose. I stood there with my stick. "Don't you hurt my Zaida!" The gander folded back his wings. Slowly. With dignity. We walked on.

"You see, *mein kind,*" Zaida said that night, "how it is? The gander wanted to stop us. All your life, there will be something or somebody who will try to stop you. But you see. You can walk by. You must be careful, though. Sometimes, where the gander stands, you should not go."

I was not careful.

I remember it clearly.

I'd been left alone to practise reading the Hebrew chants. They were boring. I started skipping pages. Zaida came back. "But, *mein kind,*" he said, pleased, "can you read so fast?" Then, "A pipsqucak! Would you do such a thing?" and, injury to insult, he tweaked my ear.

What could I do? I cried. Great sobs of self-pity and injured pride. I cried till Zaida had picked me up and was stroking my hair, "*Sha, sha.*" I cried until I saw, through my howls and my tears, that Zaida's liquid black eyes had become deeper pools of love and loneliness. I hid my face against his neck, away from those eyes, and my tears became real.

I had hurt my Zaida.

I had happened to life in a terrible way.

Blackbirds

The day I turned seven was the day I was alone with the prairie, with the light and the life of it.

It was June, 1918, and I was starting school. Papa lifted me into the buggy and handed me the reins to Fly. She looked back at me and we were off, out of the yard and onto the rolling hills of the prairie, pheasants and prairie chickens starting up out of the grasses, gophers and prairie dogs scuttling down into their holes, red-winged blackbirds on cattail perches—scarlet patches on black wings, sharp as life against the dark—calling to us.

Finally, after three wonderful miles, we came to the enormous little white school, one room with a cloakroom, a potbellied stove, and a blackboard. I was an event. I was new. I was the littlest. Everybody liked me, even the teacher in her long grey skirt and high-button blouse. I couldn't understand a thing anyone said, of course, nor they me, but it didn't make any difference. Not at first. Ulla, of summer-sky eyes and flaxen hair, Ulla Dahl whose farm was one mile down the road from us, put Fly in the barn for me. At recess, she taught me X's and O's on the blackboard. Ulla was in grade four.

But there wasn't only Ulla. There was Beth in grade one

and Bertha in grade two, two sisters with triangle faces and large grey eyes and shaggy mud-blond hair and no shoes. After that, whenever I thought of them, they were triangle shapes with grey eyes.

Everything changed because of Beth and Bertha. It was lunchtime, and we were all sitting on the front steps in the warming spring sun. Beth, the little Triangle, got up and went behind us. I felt a warm "hand" on my back. There was a giggle. Then laughter. Everyone was laughing at my back. It wasn't a hand at all. It was a foot. And now I had the print of Beth's dirty bare foot on my new sugar-sack blouse that Mama had made me just for today.

There were echoes of mean laughter in the wind as I was driving home from school.

When Ulla was there, Ulla with the light of justice in her summer-sky eyes, it wasn't so bad. It wasn't so bad, either, during school hours because then, when I was reading, the world the words made swallowed them up.

At home, Mama and I struggled over my English books together. We didn't always get it right. We read *pisnis* for *picnic,* and *coe* for *cow* . . . with each word we read wrong, there was laughter at school, mean laughter in the wind. At school, I could do nothing right: I couldn't run fast enough to be picked for steal-sticks—even my teeth, neither grey nor askew like those of the others, were found wanting.

I complained to Zaida.

"They are like the gander in the yard that wanted to stop you," he said.

"How come there are ganders every place?"

"*Mein kind,* it is life."

"Life is mean."

"No. It will make you strong."

"No, it won't. It makes you cry."

After that, Papa drove me to school, and met me, too, when Fly was being used and I had to walk home. On those walks home there were many things we didn't understand at first, but little by little, we learned to know and name: sage and cattails and prairie lilies, fossilized wood and shells, Indian hammers and arrowheads. Almost every day there was an extra treat: a little beaten path of grass, a fox run with a fox gliding by our feet; coyote puppies rolling and playing in front of their den; Mrs. Killdeer dragging a broken wing—and flying off as smart as you please when she had lured us far enough from her nest.

I told Papa everything on those walks, about Beth pulling my hair, about Ulla helping me read, about all of them throwing rocks at me when I was in the outhouse.

I didn't tell Papa about our gopher hunts. On walks with Papa, a gopher was a little tan creature with bright eyes that stood up with surprise to watch us. Papa didn't have a trap or a gun. What for? The winged and four-legged creatures had lived on the prairie before us. At school, though, the gopher wasn't anything real. It was the challenge, the pursuit, the catch, and I was as important as all the others as I carried my tin can filled with water from the slough to one of the circle of holes where the big boys stood guard waiting for the escaping prey, to kill it and cut off its tail. They—the big boys—got ten cents for each tail.

One day, I brought Papa two words to explain. There was a rare flash of anger. "I thought this was a new country."

I didn't understand.

"You won't understand."

"Not even when I get big?"

"I don't think anyone ever understands. Not even the people who use those words."

The kids at school kept saying them. And finally, one day, I understood. I understood the words, but I didn't understand why. I went home crying.

"Call them dirty Norwegians," Mama said.

"But they're not dirty."

"Neither are you."

It was the High Holidays, New Year, and I didn't have to go to school. I loved the High Holidays. Rosh Hashonah, especially, was happy—honey cake and warm honey sun slicing through the frosted harvest air, visitors and tea on the verandah. The harvest was over; there was nothing for the grownups to do but be thankful for the old year and hopeful for the new. I forgot all about the triangle shapes with grey eyes.

8

Yom Kippur was different. Yom Kippur was the Day of Atonement, the day when the grownups prayed and fasted. On Yom Kippur, we left all the grownups alone, even Zaida. On days when Zaida fasted, he also didn't smoke his pipe. It made him very growly.

I didn't think about school at all, for eight whole days, from the beginning of Rosh Hashonah until Yom Kippur a week later.

It was Tsippa, my cousin, who ruined it. Tsippa was five like Saul. But she was as different from the two of us as prunes from strawberries. She even looked different, with her red-gold hair and grey-green eyes.

We were sitting on the steps of the synagogue. Saul was picking out the raisins from his cinnamon bun and eating them first. Tsippa had picked up a small pointed rock and was scratching her arm with it. Her own arm. Quietly. Intently. She scratched until she drew blood. Then she started to cry. Aunt Sophie, black eyes flashing, was at the door. Mama was right behind her.

"Saul," Tsippa said through bitter tears, "Saul scratched me. Look!" She held out the bloody arm.

That made me mad.

"You're lying!"

She got away from me, though, even when I chased her across the prairie to the next hill, Aunt Sophie yelling behind me, "Come back here, you!" and Mama shouting from the steps of the synagogue, "Sophie, if you touch a hair of her head . . ."

"Sara!" I stopped short. It was Papa. "What's going on?" Tsippa clung to Aunt Sophie and howled.

"What's going on?" Aunt Sophie screamed an answer for me, her raven hair shaken loose and wonderful. "Your devils! One chases, the other scratches—"

"That's a lie!" I blurted out my side of the story.

Uncle Yacov turned to Tsippa. "Why, Tsippa?"

"Have you ever seen such a thing?" Aunt Sophie stormed to everyone, to anyone (by now it seemed that the whole synagogue was out there). "A father should believe his niece before his own daughter? He should love his brother more than his own wife?"

"Since when," Mama snapped, "do you compare love for a brother with love for a wife!"

9

Then Zaida spoke.

"That I should live to see such a business," he said sadly, "on Yom Kippur."

We became quiet. All of us. Yom Kippur was the day God looked at the whole year and wrote down in his book who had been good and who had been bad and who would get sick and who would live and who would die. Tsippa had been sneaky on Yom Kippur. I had chased her on Yom Kippur. What would happen?

What would happen—come to think of it—to all the kids who picked on me at school?

I looked up at the sky where Zaida had said God was. He wasn't there. He wasn't there when the kids at school were nasty, and he wasn't there now.

The next day I went back to school. Beth, the grade one Triangle, wouldn't let me in the door. "Hey!" I said, and I pulled her hair. She screamed and tried to get away, and I didn't do a thing, just held on. I held on until Teacher rang the bell and called school.

I was picked for steal-sticks that day for the first time. I was caught. Bertha put her bony hands on her skinny hips, like a long thin water bird, sneering those two words again, and "We shouldn't even play with you!"

I stamped my foot.

"You're just a bunch of dirty Norwegians!"

They stopped dead in their tracks, the whole bunch of them. "Did you hear what she said?" There was amazement in their voices, in their eyes. "Let's go tell Teacher."

Off they went, gaggling and chattering and complaining, and I wasn't even scared.

One evening when I came home, there was a woman sitting at the table, Miss McMann, pretty with rich auburn hair and brown eyes. She would be our new teacher. She would be staying with us.

By noon the first day, Beth was in the corner wearing a dunce cap. By afternoon recess, Ulla had been given the strap. Every day after that, we watched one of us being strapped or sitting in the corner wearing that cap.

Yet, at night, at home, I felt sorry for her. She would sit at the table while Mama made supper and tell Mama what she had done to us at school—and cry. The next day, at school, she would do it all over again.

Miss McMann hated us. She hated Ulla the most. Maybe because Ulla's eyes were always the most surprised by injustice. Every day, sometimes until there was blood on her knuckles, Miss McMann strapped her. But she wouldn't cry. Ulla would stand there, holding her blond head up, looking straight into Miss McMann's mud-eyes with her own summer-sky eyes, and she wouldn't cry. Sometimes, I wished she would, so Miss McMann would stop.

It was a cold blustery day, and there were cold grey wet clouds, big rolling friendly clouds that looked like they were feathering their beds and plumping their pillows so God could bounce on them. She made us go out and play. She made us stay out so long that my teeth were chattering when we came in. When she said, "Who did that?" I knew it was my teeth.

"Me, Teacher," I said. She made me spend the afternoon, the whole afternoon, on my knees. When she rang the bell to dismiss us, I fainted.

Miss McMann didn't cry at home that night. She didn't say anything.

The next day it was the same low grey clouds. Just before noon, when I was wishing I could hide in those clouds like God was, it started to snow. Not a friendly fat-snowflake snow, either. One of the fathers came to the door. "There's going to be a blizzard. You'd better close school."

But she wouldn't. He left. He took his kids with him.

Then the blizzard started, wind chasing snow, flowing sinuous white, patterns of hard white, until the white covered the hills and the world had all been taken up into the swirling white and the wind. We sat there, quiet and scared, and watched the swirling white as it tore at the school and tried to take us, too.

When school was dismissed, I didn't know what to do because Papa and Uncle Yacov were both away at an Alkali Flats Telephone Company meeting, and no one could come to get me.

"We'll go to our farm," Ulla said. "It's closest."

We went to the cloakroom for our hats and coats and

11

scarves and followed her out into the swirling white—Ulla first, me behind, then Bertha and Beth and Miss McMann. We walked and walked and walked. We walked until it was almost dark. We walked until one of us was crying. It wasn't Beth or Bertha. It was Miss McMann.

"Ulla," I said. "Miss McMann is crying."

Ulla didn't say anything. We still walked. And the crying stopped. We walked and walked—and I saw that we were following the fence around the Dahl's farm, around and around and around.

When Ulla finally led us to their barn, it was black night. Miss McMann wouldn't go any further. We went to the house and left her curled up silent and shivering in the hay.

The blizzard blew for three days while Miss McMann slept on the hay under an old buffalo robe.

When we went back to school after the winter holiday, we had a new teacher, and nobody hated me any more. Nobody hated anybody any more. We all hated Miss McMann instead. Together.

3

Sunsets

It was the summer I was nine. We were out picking eggs, Zaida and Saul and I. Suddenly, Zaida sat down on the seat of an old plough. "I can't," he said. There was surprise, then fear, in his eyes. "I can't do it any more."

After that, he sat, becoming smaller and thinner, at the window upstairs. He could see the whole yard from the window—the barn, the corral, the orchard, the pasture, the fields beyond. He could see right out to the sunset. Saul and I picked eggs on our own.

It was only when I came home from school really scared that I knew something was wrong. I had been caught cheating. My seatmate Beth and I had both been caught. We couldn't do arithmetic, either of us. We had been cheating from each other, and we had all the same wrong answers. I told Zaida about it, about being scared of the dunce cap, of being scared of being dumb, of being scared of being scared.

Zaida didn't hear. He sat looking out the window, and he hadn't heard a thing I had said.

I ran to the pasture. There was a flock of red-faced water birds with white, white feathers and black wing-tips stepping through the slough with long, elegant delicacy. Whooping

cranes. Zaida and I used to walk out there sometimes, to see
life, he said, all the wonderful different kinds of life. He would
have loved those birds.

"Sara. *Medele.* You're crying. What's the matter?"

It was Mr. Epstein, our new hired man. Mr. Epstein had left
his wife and three children and his rabbinical studies behind
in the old country. He had a thin moustache and sad eyes. Mama
said Mr. Epstein was handsome. Papa said he had book hands.
Papa teased him so much once that he got up in the middle
of the night and went out to practise stooking in the moonlight.
The whole farm had gone looking for him, dark shadows in
the silver light.

I told Mr. Epstein what the matter was.

"Your Zaida is only sick," he said. "Sometimes when we
are sick, we have time just for ourselves."

But Zaida had been sick before, and always before when
I had come to talk to him, he had smiled in his eyes.

At school the next day, Ulla had a different theory.

"That means," she said flatly, "he's going to be dead soon."

"How do you know? You don't know everything."

"Because my grandmother got like that."

"My mother, too," Bertha said.

"Just because it happened to you doesn't mean it will happen to us."

I let them play auntie-auntie-i-over by themselves.

When I went home, I went right up to Zaida's room.

"Zaida, are you going to die?"

"Where do you get such ideas?"

I told him.

He stroked my cheek.

"Everything dies, *mein kind.* Everything."

Looking through the window with Zaida that afternoon,
I tried to find something that wouldn't die—the barn, the trees,
Aunt Sophie at the clothesline—but to each, there was a nod;
only the water, the rocks, the hills, perhaps the grasses, would
remain.

"Things don't have to die," I said finally.

"Only our little hearts say that. We live to give life. And we
go to make room for the life that comes after."

"Even . . . even me?"

14

"Please God," he said, "when you are old and grey like me, you will be ready to go."

"Are you ready?"

He didn't answer. But he came downstairs for supper that night, reaching out with both hands to steady himself on the walls of the narrow staircase. He came down for supper every night after that. I still couldn't do arithmetic, though, and I was still scared. I could add and subtract anything to all my fingers and toes, but I couldn't do long multiplication or division.

Mr. Epstein found me by the slough again. I told him about arithmetic.

"Ah," he said. "This is not unusual. For me, also, the numbers were leaves in the wind until one day in my uncle's room. He was there with his friends, his books. He was holding three of his books and crying big tears. 'All these words to make the imagination sing. All the stories . . . the singing, the laughing, the crying. I must leave them behind.' 'Why, Uncle?' I asked. 'How can I carry them?' he replied through his tears. 'I have only two hands and 137 friends.' So, of course, I cried, too. My mother found both of us crying. 'You read all these books, and you can't add how much costs an onion and a potato for the soup. Go, you potato heads. Get some boxes.' 'Who will make such a big box?' my uncle asked. 'How will I carry such a big box with my two hands?' 'Ah, you are good for nothing,' my mother said. And she took out her abacus . . ."

Mr. Epstein stopped and looked at me.

"But you don't use an abacus, do you, Sara? Go. Bring a paper and a pencil."

I ran.

"Write down," he said. "Write down 137 friends. Then write down the boxes, one box for ten books . . ." and in no time at all I knew how many boxes and how many left over, and when he got a crate that could hold ten boxes, I knew it would be one crate, three boxes, and seven left over. When his mother suggested maybe he should sell those books so he would have what to eat where he was going, I knew how much money he would make if he sold them for twenty cents a book, or even $1.49.

I ran up to the house to show Zaida that I could do

15

arithmetic. The next day, I told Beth about the books and the laughing and the singing, and she could multiply and divide, too.

One afternoon when I was reading, one of the big boys picked up my desk with me in it and moved us near the wall.

"Hey!" I said.

"We're practising for the Christmas concert," he said.

"Am I going to practise, too?"

"No." Teacher answered for him.

"How come?"

"You'd better ask your mother and father. They can explain."

Mama and Papa didn't explain. They just looked at each other. Mama banged a pot down on the stove. "There's no reason for our children to be left out."

The next day I told the kids at school that we were going to have a Chanukah concert at the synagogue and that it would be in Yiddish and only people who could speak Yiddish would understand it and Chanukah lasted eight days and Christmas lasted only one so there.

But Mama ruined it. She decided something terrible, something that was going to make everybody laugh at us, mean laughter in the wind, and no one would ever forget. Saul, who hadn't even learned to talk until he was three, was going to say a poem. He'd go right up there in front of everybody and not be able to say a word, and everyone would laugh.

"But what if the kids at school come?" I wailed. "They'll laugh. Everybody will laugh."

"Don't be silly."

"Can't I stay home with Zaida?"

"He's coming, too. He's going to be honoured."

Zaida's voice floated down from upstairs.

"Am I dead that you should honour me?"

"Go tell your Zaida," Mama whispered to me, "that waiting until someone is dead to honour them is no honour."

I worried, and Zaida grumped until Mama told us we were both acting like children.

At school, I found out something else awful.

16

"Hey," Bertha giggled. "Dumb Louis says he's going to be in your play."

Dumb Louis was called *schlemiel,* good-for-nothing in Yiddish. He was tall and blond and beautiful and slow.

"Are you in it?" I asked him.

"Sure," he said. "My father's the tailor."

I confronted Mama.

"What can I do? We won't have any costumes otherwise. I don't know where we're going to get a statue, either." She sighed. "Louis will be a block of wood up there."

"*Nu?*" Zaida's voice floated down from upstairs again. "What is a statue but a block of wood?"

"You're going to be a statue," I told Louis the next day. "And everyone's going to bow down to you."

Louis smiled a beautiful slow smile all day.

"What if," I worried to Zaida that evening, "Louis moves?"

Zaida didn't hear. I followed his eyes across the yard to Papa and Uncle Yacov pitching hay from the hayloft onto the snow for the horses in the corral.

That winter, music came to our farm. Fairy-tale people— young, gentle, and in love—arrived out of the winter-blue night, and with their coming, our silent piano came to life, and the notes sang everything in the world. Each evening after supper, everybody on the farm crowded into our tiny living room as they played pictures and stories: the sparkle of a goldfinch flashing through the green leaves, the power of the hills, a hoarfrost fantasy on the windows . . . They played names I'd never heard before, names I said over and over to myself as they played: Beethoven, Bach, Liszt, Schubert.

By day, there were long serious quiet discussions, discussions of dream and hope and future. They had been sent from the old country, from Mr. Epstein's country, France, to look for places in the New World for Jews to settle. Maybe Saskatchewan, our rolling hills, would be one place. Wasn't Papa and Uncle Yacov's farm proof it was possible? Maybe—please God, why not?—their organization, the Jewish Colonization Association, would include Mr. Epstein's wife and babies among them.

I didn't tell anyone at school about the music, not even Ulla.

17

It was a secret, a secret that made me feel as big and light inside as the sky. It was a secret for whenever there was mean laughter in the wind.

The night of the concert was a clear cold thirty-below night, the kind of night when the stars are clear prism-points of emerald and sapphire light, and it seems like all you have to do is reach out to pluck one and have it glowing and flashing in your hand. We all piled into the cutter under the horsehair blanket, the footwarmer at our feet, Papa flicked the reins, and we were sliding over the blue-night snow, leaving ribbons behind us. I wanted to never get there.

Everybody was there. Our piano was there. Ulla was there. Bertha and Beth were there. I pretended I didn't see them. I knew they were going to laugh at Saul. All the time that Good-for-Nothing-Block-of-Wood Louis was being bowed down to, all during the time that Hannah's seven sons were being killed for refusing to bow down, even while Mr. Epstein was telling the story of Chanukah in Yiddish and Uncle Yacov was translating to English—through all that, I was locked in my own little bubble of fear: I saw Saul—all of us—being laughed at. Only the singing notes of the piano penetrated.

Suddenly—

"If he is rude and ungracious, I'll never forgive him."

It was Mama. She was looking at Zaida. Papa was helping him to a chair at the front so the farmers could honour him.

And, as they spoke, I saw not the tired eyes of my grandfather, but the snapping black eyes of the younger man who had followed his determined young sons to Canada in 1905. I saw him hunched at the kitchen table, a pencil carefully held in his large hand as he drew the plans for the synagogue: how much space for the congregation that would one day fill it, how much space for the stage, where should be the room for the *siddurum* and the teaching books for the children . . . I saw him walking to each new farm across the virgin prairie wool, saw him pulling at his beard as he argued: "A land of snow and wolves . . . no synagogue . . . One day, you will marry. Like this, will your children be Jews?" I saw him sleeping under a silent moon guarding the site, his snores part of a symphony of crickets, owls, frogs, coyotes, mosquitoes. In his reply, I saw my grandfather as he cajoled and charmed those promises of work: "It was Aaron's dream, this colony—Jews owning land like other men. Fifteen years ago, you were just boys, all of you, building your barns, picking rocks, ploughing fields. I was an old man with nothing to do. I cooked, I cleaned for my sons, and every new Jew who came along, I fed, and bothered with the synagogue." He started down the aisle, and, with the shrug so characteristic of Papa, with Uncle Yacov's tease— "But in my shoes, you—all of you—who wouldn't do the same?"

Then—please God, don't let it be—Saul, a small straight figure with Papa's blue-black hair and Mama's fair eyes walking up to that stage in front of everyone. He walked like he knew exactly what he was doing, and said his poem, gesturing in all the right places like he knew exactly what he was saying:

> As a rule, man's a fool.
> When it's hot, he wants it cool.
> When it's cool, he wants it hot,
> Always wanting what is not.
> Therefore, as a rule, man's a fool.

There was laughter, laughter, laughter—laughter that rolled right into me and filled me with love and tears. And Louis hadn't moved. Not once.

As we jingled home over luminous snow, I thought about Ulla and Beth and Bertha playing *driedle* for raisins and walnuts with us; I thought about everybody understanding the play even though it was in Yiddish.

Magic happened then, the magic of a snowflake, a single snowflake drifting down out of the night. I watched it come down, floating down to me, a gift like a star. I put out my hand to catch it, and it drifted onto my mitten, lay there glittering.

And a second one, floating, drifting onto Saul's mitten. Two perfect snowflakes glittering different perfect points on our mittens.

"We are all children of the sky," Zaida said softly. "Even me, with my old broken points."

The first snowflake melted. Then the second.

"Ah. You see?" he said.

"*Medele.*" It was Mr. Epstein. I was down by the slough watching the water sparkle blue jewels in the sunlight and two

19

Canada Geese making ripples in it. "Before you is the richest man in the universe. I have a letter . . ." He opened it ceremoniously, cleared his throat, prepared to speak—and broke into joyous tears. "Three years since I have seen my babies," he smiled through the tears. "They are coming."

I went to tell Zaida. He heard. He smiled.

I sat at the window with him. The sun was setting crimson and lemon and streaks of green against the pale stubble of the harvested fields, crimson and yellow and streaks of green behind Mr. Epstein as he brought his hayrack full of sheaves of wheat off the fields. The harvesters would soon be gone, all of them, the round one who ate and ate and never talked, not even to say, "Pass the peas, please," but stood up and took the bowl instead; and the white-haired boy whose hair had turned white overnight in the war—they would be gone, and it would just be us again. Mr. Epstein and us. He had climbed onto the platform of the separator. He was singing out his letter to the round man waiting with his hayrack, to the white-haired boy pitching the sheaves into the separator from a second hayrack . . .

All of a sudden, the world stopped. The platform Mr. Epstein was standing on had split. He disappeared into the cutting knives below.

When they pulled him out, he was bloody and still. The smiling part of him was gone. Like the cat.

"My God," Zaida pleaded, raising his arms to heaven. "My God, how can this be? You will have me soon, isn't that enough?"

Then I knew.

"You lied! You said you weren't dying. You lied, you lied, you lie—"

"*Mein kind.* Sarela." I looked into eyes that were pools of pain and silence. "I lied to myself."

I knew the next day, too. Walking home from school, I knew.

I went up to Zaida's room. His eyes were closed like he was trying to sleep. He looked tired. Not restful. Not peaceful. Tired. So, so tired.

My Zaida was dead, and I didn't cry. Not till a long time after when I was watching the sunset scarlet and gold caught in the ice-glass that was forming over the dark water of the slough. The wind fell, and in the sudden large silence, I seemed to hear Mr. Epstein's excited voice—"*Medele*"—then there was Zaida's gentle hand on my hair, and his voice, no longer tired: "We live to give life. We come . . . we sparkle . . . and we go."

That made me mad. Mr. Epstein's babies were coming. What about them? He wasn't ready to go. He never even wanted to be a farmer. If Canada had let him in as a rabbi, it wouldn't have happened. And what about me and Saul? We weren't ready for Zaida to go.

I threw a rock at the scarlet and gold sunset colours in the ice in the slough. It cracked, and the dark water welled up over the shining colours.

4

Beth

The summer I was eleven was a bad dream with Beth and the dentist and Chicken George and the bootleggers all mixed up in it. It even started in the middle of the night.

Something from outside had scared me awake. It wasn't the crying of the twin baby girls. From my window, I saw in the black night the lights of two cars going right for each other, splashing through the spring mud for each other's headlight eyes. Saul was right beside me. "They're playing chicken," he said, big-eyed and excited. "I bet they're bootleggers." We watched until one car hit the other, and Papa and Uncle Yacov went out to talk to them, and Mama came up to remind us we had to go to school the next day. "Gee," Saul said. "Wait till I tell the other kids."

The next day, Beth listened to Saul bragging about the bootleggers playing chicken in our yard. She turned to me with that old sneer. "Your Pa! What a smart aleck! Nobody else's Pa would go out in the middle of them bootleggers. He acts like he's the King."

"He does not!"

"Well, that's what my Pa says, and he says he knows your Pa real good, about as good as a hog knows a sow."

"Okay, if you don't believe me, we'll go to Ulla's after school and ask her. Mr. Dahl knows my father real good, too."

Ulla didn't come to school any more, not since she had finished grade eight two years before, and I often went over after school. As soon as she saw someone coming up the road for a visit, even if it was only Saul bringing something for Mrs. Dahl from Mama, she'd start making a Cake In A Hurry. By the time Beth and I got to the door—with our arms full of butter-cups and yellow lady's-slippers—the cake was almost out of the oven.

"Guess what!" Ulla said before either Beth or I could say a word. "Four of my cousins are coming from Norway to live with us! And Britt, the oldest, is my age! Papa's gone to Alkali Flats to get lumber to build another room."

"These aren't all for me!" Mrs. Dahl said. She set the flowers into small pickling jars. "You are still pressing flowers for your science project, I think."

"And do you know what else?" Ulla said. "Carl came to visit me."

We didn't know who Carl was.

"He works for Sonnergren's. He's tall, and he has brown hair, and he's almost as strong as Papa, and he's Norwegian like us. He got into a fight last week."

Mr. Dahl had just come in. He was in a bad mood.

"Is trouble-makers all over the world. Is people called Ku Klux Klan in Weyburn, and they think we are stupid, too."

And that's all he would say.

"Does my father think he's smarter than anybody else?" I asked Ulla when the three of us were finally alone.

"I don't know."

"Yes, you do. You're my friend."

"I can't say if I don't know."

"How would you like it," I demanded, "if I said that about your father?"

She was silent.

I walked home by myself, and I clumped right through the patches of buttercups.

It wasn't long after that that I had to go to Estevan to see the dentist. Saul used Fly and the buggy to drive me to Alkali Flats, and I took the train from there. I loved the train, all big and black and huffing and puffing and full of places it had been, and places it was going to.

Estevan was the place Papa had come first when he came to Canada from Austria. Estevan was only a few houses then, he said, and a railroad station and a hotel and a restaurant and a dray and a shoemaker. Now, it had wide streets and cement sidewalks and ice-cream-cone streetlights and a coal mine and a synagogue and churches and a high school and big train stations for each of the CPR and CNR railroads. Sometimes, when the snow was gone, and Papa had taken the tin lizzie, the Model T, off the blocks again, Papa and Mama drove into Estevan to do business. We'd all be up early, and, as soon as the chores were done, we'd pile into the tin lizzie, and three hours later, Saul and I would be skipping down the street, each with our nickel to buy an ice-cream cone.

When I went to Estevan by myself, I got to take the train. But I had to stay overnight at the Isreals' boardinghouse because there wasn't a train back until the next day. I hated staying there. As soon as you put out the light, there'd be bedbugs, little red bitey bedbugs. Mrs. Isreals, a grey-haired pillow-shaped lady, washed and scrubbed and cleaned all day, but there were still those bitey bedbugs. She used to cry about those bedbugs.

I hated going to the dentist, too. His office was painted green, the same green every place you hate is painted, and there was a rude sign as soon as you opened the door:

> My friend did come and I did trust him
> I lost my friend and I lost my custom
> To lose my friend it grieves me sore
> So I've resolved to trust no more.

But he was handsome, as handsome as a movie star, with ice-blue eyes and black hair slicked down and shiny. He moved slow, like he was used to people watching him. He was never in a hurry.

"I hear," he said, sticking the drill into my mouth, "they're going to get that Jew." He said it in a way that went right to my stomach. As soon as I got out of his office, I was sick all over the sidewalk.

On the train on the way home, there was a little man in a brown suit who spoke Yiddish. "*Nu?*" he said. He sounded like Zaida. "Where are you going all alone? Whose daughter are you?" I told him. "Ah, the Schiller brothers," he said. "The farmers. They have a good name. In my family, we were inn-keepers in the old country. We had the name of our business even, Bronfman. *Bronfin* is *liquor* in Yiddish. To have the name of your business, it must be your family has been in it for a long time, *nu?*" There weren't so many things a Jew was allowed to do in the old country. Here, we own land, we vote, we go to school. We live like human beings. It is not a small thing to live like a human being. Your father, for instance, a justice of the peace, not just a farmer. In the old country, who ever heard of a Jew a justice of the peace?" I asked him if the inns in the old country had bedbugs like Mrs. Isreals'. He said inns all over the world had bedbugs. If you didn't want to hunt down each bug personally, you had to burn down the house and the mat-tresses and start over. Then I told him about the dentist. "People like that," he said, "are all talk. They don't hurt you. Not even the Ku Klux Klan. Not here."

I would have forgotten all about him except for the man having tea in the kitchen when Saul and I got back from the station. He was wearing a red and green checked jacket, and he was round with round red cheeks, and a gold watch chain across his little round stomach, and a cigar in his little round fingers. Aunt Sophie was in a going-to-town dress, but Papa and Uncle Yacov were in their dusty overalls and Mama was in a housedress. One of the twins was trying to stand on Papa's lap. Mama was holding the other one. There was flour on her cheek.

"I've got a proposition for you folks," the man was saying. He poked at the air with his cigar. "If you listen to me, you could be rich. You could give up farming. By this time next year—"

We waited. He picked a walnut out of his pocket and cracked it.

"—you'll be sitting in Winnipeg with your feet up."

"Is that so!" Uncle Yacov said. "Let's hear your proposition."

"Whiskey," the man said. "Nothing illegal in it. Making whiskey and shipping it—it's legal in this country. We're in the business of shipping it. That's all."

"Across the line," Papa pointed out.

"Where it's plenty illegal," Uncle Yacov added. "And plenty trouble, too."

"No, sir! The American boys pick it up here. They're the ones who get into trouble."

"So I guess it wasn't your men shooting off their guns in our yard the other night?"

"No, sir! Not my boys. My boys don't carry guns. Must have been the boys from across the line." He cracked another nut. "You boys have a good name around here. I'll make you boys a proposition. Let us use your name. You don't have to come in with us. Just let us use your name, and we'll cut you in."

"If you use our name," Uncle Yacov said, "what good will it be to us?"

"Don't your families deserve better than this?" He was starting to look white and mean. "What kind of life is it? Is this a life? Slaves to cows and horses? Your wives—" He stopped. Both babies started to cry. "And your kids! What kind of future is it?"

"Look," Papa said. His jaw was tight. "I know we're close to the border. I'm sure you like that even more than our name. But we've got a farm to run." He got up. "Whatever you're doing, you can do without us."

The man left.

"There was a man on the train," I said. "He said the same thing."

I told them about him and the "good name."

"It was Sam Bronfman on the train," Aunt Sophie said. "A man like this will always be all right, a Mr. Alrightnik. He's smart to work for Sam Bronfman. Why should we say no so fast? Why shouldn't we talk to him first?"

"What for?" Mama snapped. "So he can spit on us, too?"

"But he's not like that—' and I told them about Bronfman coming from *bronfin* and about people living like human beings. I asked what the Ku Klux Klan was. They were people

26

who hated everybody except themselves, Mama said—Catholics, Jews, Negroes, Indians—they were people who tried to blame their problems on everyone else.

Later that week, Uncle Yacov was away at a meeting about the railroad lobby. On those nights, I stayed with Aunt Sophie and she would make Tsippa and me anything we wanted, even doughnuts, and tell us stories about the old country—the wise men of Chelm who thought the moon was more important than the sun because it shone at night when you really needed it; her father's store with all kinds of silk ribbons and wool cloth; the pogrom in her village and how it took two weeks to bury all the bodies afterwards; the evil spirit that lurked behind every bush and door and spoke in every breath of wind . . .

When I stayed with Aunt Sophie, I had to sleep with her, but on the outside, so that if the devil came, she said, he would get me first.

Suddenly, one night, I was jerked awake.

"Your father, the big shot!"

Aunt Sophie sounded just like Beth, just like the dentist.

"Why? What do you mean?"

"Schiller is such a wonderful name? I'll die on this farm for that name. Does Yacov ever listen to me? Everybody—your father, your mother with her reading and her writing—everybody knows better than me. Even in the old country, who lived on a farm?"

"Papa says Jews have to get out of the old country."

"Papa! Aaron this, Aaron that! I'll kill him one day, as I live, I will!"

It was a long time before she stopped talking. Later that night, I woke up screaming from a dream with Beth and Aunt Sophie and the dentist and the bootleggers in it. I thought Papa was dead. I scared the living daylights out of Aunt Sophie. She made me go home. In the moonlight, the yard was quiet and peaceful. Only friendly spirits came out in the moonlight.

The next day, I was in the kitchen writing a letter for Papa when I heard Mama and Papa arguing in the bedroom. It was the chickens. After Zaida died, Mama wrote to the University of Saskatchewan to try out different breeds: white Leghorns (not enough meat), red Buff Orpingtons (not enough eggs), and, finally, the grey and white Barred Rocks (enough of both). Then she made Papa build chicken coops so the chickens would all lay their eggs in one place, and so they would be safe from hawks and weasels. Nevertheless, in spite of her chicken coops, the chickens were disappearing. Constable Semeniuk had discovered why, but Papa wouldn't press charges.

"The man is alone with five children," Papa was saying. "Who is going to feed his family if he goes to jail?"

"But, Aaron, he caught Chicken George with twenty-five of my chickens."

"Eva . . ." Papa was upset. "Beth and Bertha are Sara's friends. If I put him in jail for trying to feed his family, what am I going to say to her?"

"Just wait," I thought to myself. "Wait till I get her!"

The next day, I got her.

"Your father's a thief! A chicken thief!"

Beth didn't say a word. She just looked at me with storm-grey eyes—with enough hate to start a prairie fire. Then she slapped me. Hard. And turned her back and walked across the prairie away from the school.

That year was the first time we had our long holiday in the summer instead of the winter. (You didn't start school the day of your birthday any more, either. You had to wait till September.) There was to be an ice-cream social that summer, after the crops were in and before the haying, to raise money for the railroad. If the lobby was successful, either the CPR or the CNR would send a spur down from one of their main lines and the train might pass only a mile from our farm. It would take only one hour to take a wagonload of grain to the elevator and back, instead of three hours to Alkali Flats like it did now. Ulla was coming over to help me cook the custard for the ice-cream. We were making it with the ice from last winter, ice cut from the slough and stored in the ice-house that Saul had found a pattern for in *The Western Producer* the year before.

"Is Beth coming to help?" Ulla asked.

"I haven't seen her since she stopped coming to school," I said.

"How come?"

I shrugged.

"They're crazy," Ulla said. "The whole family is crazy. Do you know what Chicken George is doing now? He's suing my father."

"Why? What did your father do?" I asked.

"Nothing," she said.

"How do you know?"

"He's my father."

"So?" I said.

Ulla wouldn't talk to me.

"I'm just being fair," I said.

"You are not."

"I can't say if I don't know."

The day of the social, the Dahls walked over at seven in the morning with their nieces and nephews, rusty-haired, blue-eyed, freckled, and—except for Britt—smiling. Their arms were full of jars of lemonade and Ulla's Cakes In a Hurry. They all had new clothes Mrs. Dahl had made, dresses for the girls, yellow voile with giant pink and blue flowers—blue like their eyes—and shirts for the boys, blue and white checks. The only English words they knew were "thank you," "good-day," and "ice-cream."

The men went to trim branches off the trees to lay on the roof of the bowery they had built for the dance. The women started setting boards on chairs for tables and laying tablecloths and setting out dishes.

By ten o'clock, people were arriving in tin lizzies and buggies and wagons, the women in short cotton dresses and cloche hats, the men in suits and ties and stiff collars. By noon, everybody was there, from as far away as Estevan, from Westby across the line, the Alkali Flats Citizens' Band with their drums and trumpets and French horns, Dr. Lowe and Mrs. Lowe and quiet blond Angela, every farmer for thirty miles around . . . Chicken George and Bertha and her little brothers and sisters were there. Beth wasn't.

For the first time, I felt awful about her, and it went right to my stomach, like at the dentist's. The sweet perfume of the cakes I was cutting (there were a million of them, and half of them were Aunt Sophie's) started to make me sick. When Tsippa came up to me—'As soon as there's a town, we'll move off this farm and have a store!"—I snapped at her: "You're as crazy as your mother!" But I shouldn't have, because she went straight to Aunt Sophie, and Aunt Sophie went screaming to Mama, and Mama came to me. "For heaven's sake, Sara, go apologize, or we'll never have any peace."

I did.

But while I was saying it, I remembered what Aunt Sophie had said about Papa, and I remembered the dreams. I was lying when I said it.

I went to find Ulla. It was hot. July hot. By now, the men had taken off their jackets and rolled up their sleeves, and the women were sitting on blankets in the shade of the orchard beside sleeping babies and empty picnic baskets. Ulla was on the verandah with her cousin Britt and her father and Dr. Lowe and Angela. Even though Angela and I were almost the same age, I had never heard her speak. Mama said she was shy.

"By jumpin'," Mr. Dahl was saying. He said it with a y. "By yumpin'," he said. "He sells me his roan, and the next minute, by yumpin' if he isn't back at my door with a story as long as your arm to get it back, and when I think he is yoking me, by yumpin', if he isn't back with a story to sue me, telling me I'm starving my own horse."

"A roan," Dr. Lowe said. "When was that exactly?"

Mr. Dahl told him. Dr. Lowe threw back his head and laughed, a big explosive laugh all over the yard.

"Why, I'll be darned if he didn't try to sell me the same horse the very next day! And at a higher price, too!"

They called Papa over and told him the same story. Papa didn't say a word. He just went to find Chicken George. Ulla and I followed. Angela stayed with her father. Dr. Lowe was still laughing.

"Now, look," Papa said to Chicken George. Chicken George listened, his eyes narrowed, blinking like a chicken in the sun. "No, sir," he stretched his neck in protest. "That ain't it, that ain't it a-tall."

"Look," Papa said. "If you sue Thor, Dr. Lowe is willing to testify against you. As a matter of fact, Thor's got a pretty good case to sue you right now. If I were you, I'd go right over there and apologize."

"I ain't apologizin'!" Chicken George turned white. "Not for somethin' he done."

"Thor would starve himself before he'd let one of his animals go hungry, and you know it." He took Chicken George's arm and led him to the verandah.

"George has come to apologize," Papa said to Mr. Dahl. "He says even if he won the case, he'd lose a friend for life. Isn't that right, George?"

Chicken George nodded, blinked and nodded.

"I was just saying to George," Papa said. "I've seen men— they sue each other, and then they never speak again. But when they agree out of court, why, they're friends for life." They sat down on the verandah. "There aren't so many of us out here that we can afford to lose friends."

"So what do you think of my father now?" I asked Ulla.

We were sitting on the verandah steps eating melted ice-cream and crumbs from all the cakes mixed together. "Do you still think my Papa thinks he's better than anybody else?"

"I never said that. Beth did."

"You agreed."

"No, I didn't. I said I didn't know. Friends don't say things just because you want them to. That's lying."

"I think I did something awful," I said.

"What?"

I told her what I had said to Beth.

She thought for a minute. "Mama always says children don't have to get involved in the ridiculous things their parents do. Maybe it was your mother and father's business."

"She started it."

"I know." Then she said, "Maybe you should tell her you're sorry."

"But I only said the truth."

"You can still be sorry."

That night, the full moon was shining through the leaves of the bowery, and Ulla was dancing in it, dancing in the moonlight with Carl, and the leaf-shadow patterns lay over the flowers on the dress. I was only eleven. I watched.

31

At midnight, the band stopped playing for lunch. Mr. Dahl went up to the front.

"Where are the boys? Get the boys."

They got them. It was Papa and Uncle Yacov.

"What do you think?" Mr. Dahl asked everyone. "Did we raise enough money? Can Yacov go to Ottawa?"

There were yeses, and well-I-guesses, and by yumpin's, and stop your foolings.

"By yumpin'," Mr. Dahl said. "By yumpin', Yacov will go to Ottawa, and he will come back on our railroad."

Aunt Sophie looked at Papa standing at her husband's side. There was prairie-fire hate in her eyes. Beth's prairie-fire hate. "Look at Aaron," she said. "Yacov should be with his wife at a time like this. I'll break them up if it's the last thing I do."

That fall, I had to go to the dentist again. This time I didn't want to get on the train, not to go see the dentist. And he did it again. He walked toward me, slowly, with his ice-blue eyes and slicked down black hair, and stuck the drill into my mouth. "I hear they're going to get that Jew."

This time, I pushed his hand away.

"I'm Jewish, too, you know."

"Oh, I didn't mean—"

"You did. You did mean it."

I left his green office.

And I wasn't sick after.

Mama was going to be mad, though. They had paid all that money for the train and for Mrs. Isreals and I was still going to have my toothache, and I had been rude to an adult.

On the train the next day, I heard the conductor talking about it. "That Jew" had been shot, "that Jew" with the diamond tie-pin as big as an apple. "That Jew" had been shot—and it served him right.

Both Papa and Uncle Yacov were waiting for me with warm hugs and worried eyes. Everywhere we went—the hotel for coffee, Billy Frank's for the mail, the Weyburn Security Bank— "that Jew" was all anyone talked about. He had watered down the whiskey, they said. No, they said, it was shipped straight from Vancouver. How could he have watered it? The railroad was in on it, they said. Two men had been drinking in the hotel in Bienfait, they said, drinking all afternoon waiting for him, waiting with their guns. There are laws, Papa said; we can't afford to take the law into our own hands.

"How come," I asked on the way home, "if everybody knew somebody was going to shoot him, nobody told him?"

Papa and Uncle Yacov looked at me, looked at each other.

"How come, if everybody saw those men drinking, nobody caught them after?"

They still didn't answer.

"Tsippa says we're rich. Are they going to shoot us, too?"

Mama took one look at me and put me to bed. When I woke up, it was quiet and dark. Mama and Papa were talking in the kitchen.

"Just wait," Mama was saying. "No one will ever admit to knowing those two men who shot him. Look at the pogroms in the old country. Is anyone ever convicted of killing a Jew? Is anyone ever convicted of killing a dog? Wait. There'll never be a conviction."

"This is a new world, Eva," Papa said. But he didn't say it the way he had said it to Chicken George. He didn't say it as if he believed it.

"Yes. This is a new world. The Ku Klux Klan is in this new world."

In my dream that night, Papa was still dead, and so was Uncle Yacov and the little man on the train. I woke up crying. Mama was sitting on my bed. I told her about Beth and the dentist and Papa and Chicken George and "that Jew."

"Everybody hates everybody," I said.

"Never mind the dentist," she said. "You did right."

"But what about all the other people?"

"I don't know," she said. "I don't always understand why people make life so hard for each other."

"Was Beth wrong, too?"

"Yes. She was. But it doesn't mean you can't be sorry for what you did."

I took Fly and the buggy to Beth's farm the next day, and I practised all the way. The geese and ducks honked from a blue sky on their way south, the rabbits perked up their ears as we rattled by—and I practised saying I was sorry.

5

Little Girls

"When did you find out about sex?"

I looked up. It was the girl sitting in front of me, and— except for her blond hair and blue-grey eyes—it was like looking into a mirror, both of us with small mouths and noses, both of us with Buster Brown haircuts, both of us in grey Eaton's catalogue long-sleeved V-necked sweaters.

"What?" I said.

"Never mind. I'll ask you after. Do you want to go walking after school?"

As soon as the bell rang, she turned around again.

"I bet you're boarding at Roitman's, and I bet your school only had up to grade eight, didn't it?"

"How did you know?"

"Oh, I know everything. Let's go."

She took my arm and steered me out of the school and down the street. "This is Billy Frank's post office. He sells *True Stories* and post cards. Papa says they're the work of the devil. And this is the Weyburn Security Bank, and the dray, and Dr. Lowe lives over there behind, and there's the lumber yard and the Roitman's hotel that belongs to the people you're staying with, and—"

"This isn't the first time I've ever been to Alkali Flats," I said.
"It isn't?"
"No. I came in every week."
"What for?"
"For piano lessons at Mrs. Lowe's, and so Saul could get the mail and do errands for Papa, and so we could get the groceries from the Schwartz's after."

Her eyes were wide, wide and grey now with the low grey clouds behind her. "Gee, my father would never let me go to town if I wasn't going to school. He doesn't let my mother come, ever."

"Does he let you say 'Gee?' I thought that was taking Jesus's name in vain."

By that time, we were walking along the railroad tracks past the four elevators, a yellow Imperial elevator, a green Long Creek Grain elevator, a white Ogilvy Milling Company elevator, and an orange United Grain Growers elevator. We were near the edge of the slough, a dead slough—no trees, no birds, no cattails—an alkali slough with the white crusted alkali around the edges. Under the grey sky, it was like a dead eye. Behind us, we could look back and see the elevators, high as mountains on the flat, and see the cluster of stores—the pool hall, Lee Hing's cafe, the United Church, the liquor store . . .

"Do you like it?" I asked.
"What?"
"Living with a whole bunch of houses."
"I don't know. We live on a farm, too. My father says he would never live in spitting distance of anybody, not even the King."

She pointed out to the flat, the true flat, where it feels like the world goes on forever. I saw in the distance, past the dead slough, a house, a small barn, a granary, and no trees. Not one.

"It's not very pretty here, is it?" I said.
"Why, where do you come from?"
"Twelve miles south of here. Only we have hills. Papa says only the railroad would be stupid enough to put a town on alkali that even the gophers are smart enough to stay away from."

"Do you have your monthlies?"
"Yes."

35

"I don't. And I don't care because then I can't have babies, and who wants babies."

"Everybody."

"They're messy. And they're always crying."

"No, they're not. They're cute, and they learn to talk."

"Anyway, it doesn't matter, because only bad girls have babies when they're not married, and I'm never going to get married. Alkali Flats has a lot of bad girls. Every time you turn around. They're a dime a dozen."

I asked Mrs. Roitman that evening.

"Are there lots of girls who have babies and aren't married in Alkali Flats?"

"No, why?"

"Nora says bad girls are a dime a dozen."

"Oh, dear," she said. Mrs. Roitman was like a little blond *knaidel*. Mr. Roitman was, too, but he looked like a giant beside her. "I think you'd better ask your mother."

I went to the Roitman's hotel to use the telephone. The clerk at the front desk pointed—through the bar where two farmers were drinking beer, through the restaurant where another farmer was eating pie and drinking coffee and reading the *Morning Leader*—to the kitchen. I pushed open the door.

"Hello, sugah."

She was tall with the light of the sunset green in her eyes, and skin like cream, and a long, long braid down her back. I stared.

"You-all lookin' for a little somethin' to eat?"

"I'm looking for the telephone. Mrs. Roitman said to ask Janine."

"Ah'm Janine, and that there's the telephone."

She nodded at the wall behind my head. She was rolling pie dough, moving with the suppleness of wheat before the wind. "You-all do your talkin', and ah'll slip you a piece of my walnut pie just waitin' for a young lady to exclaim over."

I picked up the receiver and rang Mama, two long and one short.

"Mama," I said. "Are there girls who aren't married and have babies in Alkali Flats? Nora says they're a dime a dozen."

Mama gasped.

"Sara! We don't talk about those things on the telephone! People listen!" Then, "Papa will come for you on Friday." She rang off.

I put the receiver back on the hook. There was a piece of buttery-sugary walnut pie waiting for me—pecan pie, she said, without the pecans. "How does little Nora Jensen know so much about bad girls?"

"Nora knows everything. She says bad girls are a dime a dozen."

Janine laughed, a big, rich wonderful laugh. She laughed and laughed. Then she said, "Sugah, the only thing the Lord give us plenty of out here is the wind and the birds in the spring."

"My mother says we've got the most beautiful sky in the world, and she should know, she came all the way from the old country."

"I declare!"

"And she says we've got beautiful flowers and room to grow and not one of her children is dead. In the old country, her mother was sick, and when she woke up from the fever, five of her children were dead. That's when they moved here, so no more of their children would die. Do you know any bad girls?"

She shook her head.

On the way home, it was the first thing I asked Papa. He turned and looked at me, a long look, and then, scratching his head, "You'd better ask your mother."

I asked her.

Mama brushed the hair off her forehead with the back of her hand and looked out the window.

"You're a big girl," she said, "and we can't always be there to protect you. You're going to have to make up your own mind about who your friends are. But I guess," she sighed, "I'd better tell you."

So she told me. Sex was for two people who loved each other. Nevertheless, some women gave men sex for money. Prostitutes. Some girls didn't sell it, but had sex before they were married, and girls had to be careful, because they could

37

let their feelings get away from them. Anybody could be that kind of bad girl.

Nora was waiting for me outside of the Lowe's after my lesson. She had her back to me. "Guess what?" she said.
"What?"
She turned around.
"Nora! You're wearing lipstick!"
"Smell me." She stuck her ear under my nose. It was a smell like every flower from spring to fall mashed together. It was awful.
"That's perfume," she said. "That's what Chautauqua girls wear. Come on. Let's walk out on the highway, and then you can put some on, and we can roll our stockings."
She drew a lipstick mouth on me, a gooey sticky mouth. We looked at ourselves in the water in the ditch, saw ourselves, twin Buster Brown heads, one fair, one dark, against a blue heaven, saw red mouths on our twin heads, red as blood.
"Gee," Nora said. "We're beautiful. Papa says lipstick is the agent of the devil."
"Maybe it is," I said, "because every time the Chautauqua girl comes to the farm to get Papa to pledge, Mama and Papa have a big fight."
Nora was all eyes, limpid blue reflections of a limpid sky. "No kidding? How come?"
"Mama says Papa falls for any sales pitch from a pretty face, even a painted one."
"My father would make Mama pray on her knees for a week if she said that to him, sure as shooting."
"Not mine. He just shrugs, and then he explains. He says the Chautauquas bring culture to small communities, and they've been doing it for twenty years across the line, and now they've come into Canada by way of the West, and we'll be ahead of the East. And Mama says, 'You and your ahead of the East.'"
"And he still doesn't get mad?"
I shook my head. "He laughs. He says, 'I don't know what you're so upset about, you're pretty, too.'"
"Gee. That's romantic."
"No, it isn't. Mama gets really mad then."

"Who'd be crazy enough to get mad if someone thought they were pretty?"

"Mama says she's not pretty."

"Quick! Duck down! Here comes a car!"

There was a shy half-moon shining on me through my window that night, shining on Nora and me. I could see Nora's farm from my window. I felt like the moon, afraid to come out. What would Mama and Papa say if they found out that Nora and I had rolled our stockings and painted our faces?

"Is it true," I asked Janine the next time I was at the hotel, "that only bad girls paint their faces?"

She put down the corn she was shucking. "Now, let me see. Is it true that people who laugh are always happy?"

"I guess so," I said.

"No, now don't 'guess so,' sugah. Think. You-all never seen people laugh at different times? Like when they're so mad they don't know what else to do? There are plenty of times a person laughs, and they're cryin' inside. So. Tell me. You been wearin' paint on your face?"

"Just when I go walking with Nora. We buy it from the Avon lady."

"Well, I don't see nothin' bad about you, sugah. Must be somethin' else that makes a body good or bad."

I could hardly wait to tell Nora that we weren't bad. I was so happy, I almost cried.

Then it happened.

I fell in love.

He was tall and blond and blue-eyed. I saw him as soon as Saul and I drove into the yard that Friday evening. He was standing at the watering trough, watering his horse. He was talking to Papa about buying some cattle for his father. I drank him in with my eyes. His name was Bruce.

"We can't sell to you," Papa was saying. "You're across the line."

"But we're only four miles from you. If you want to sell up here, you'll have to go three times as far, and only get half as much. Our prices for wheat and cattle are twice as high as up here, you know. You'd be crazy not to sell."

He stayed for supper, and they talked about it some more, until Mama said, "Aaron—it's illegal," and, "Sara, you're not eating."

The tall blond cowboy left in the moonlight on his gleaming brown horse with the braided tail.

"What's wrong with you?" Nora asked.

"Nothing."

"Yes, there is. You're moony."

"I am not."

I went to see Janine.

"Am I moony?"

"Why? You-all in love?"

"I think so."

"Tell me about him."

I told her everything.

"Is that all?"

"Yes. Except he gets in fights at all the picnics and dances."

"Then why you in love with him?"

"I don't know. People don't know why they're in love. It's magic. Besides, maybe he doesn't do that any more. That was last year. He was just a kid."

"Don't you have anybody nice out your way?"

"There's the man who sent a picture of him sitting on his tin lizzie in front of his shack. He wants to marry me. And a skinny man from New York. Ulla says he has a crush on me."

"You're only fourteen."

"I know. Besides, I love Bruce."

Nora and I were out walking again, twins in our brown Eaton's catalogue coats with the fox collars. All of a sudden, she grabbed my arm and pulled me off the sidewalk to the other side of the street.

"I thought you wanted to go to Billy Frank's to look at *True Stories*," I said.

"You don't want to walk on the same side as her, do you?" It was Beth. She had changed. With her hair short and fluffy, the light of the sun in ash-blond waves, the grey eyes in a

40

delicate triangle face, she was simply lovely. "She sleeps with men."

"How do you know?"

"Everybody knows except you. You're so dumb."

"You don't know anything about Beth! Her mother is dead, and her father—" I stopped.

"Why don't you talk to her if you're so smart."

"Because," I said. "She won't talk to me."

And I wouldn't talk about it any more.

I asked Janine.

"Does Beth sleep with men?"

"Chicken George's little girl? She comes in with one of the travellers sometimes."

"Does she do it for money?"

Her eyes flashed jade green. "Your Nora could try the patience of a saint! You tell her what she doin' to Beth is ten times worse than anything that child ever goin' to do to anyone but herself. When a child's unlucky and young as she, she doin' it because she needin' love."

When Papa came to get me, I told him what Nora and Janine had said. His jaw tightened. "I'll get Constable Corrigan after him. He's going to have to do his travelling somewhere else." For almost the whole rest of the trip, he talked about men like that who have wives and daughters and sisters at home and go around picking on other men's wives and daughters and sisters.

I told Nora.

"So there," I said. "It wasn't a whole bunch, it was only one, and it's not her fault. A man his age should know better than to pick on defenceless young girls."

The next time I used the telephone at the hotel, Nora was outside waiting for me.

"How come you never tell me anything Janine says?"

"Like what?"

"Like where she's from and what she's doing here."

"She doesn't tell me. Anyway, you don't ask questions. People have come here from all over the world to start over, and why they've come is none of our business."

"Who said?"

"My mother."

"She doesn't know what people say about Janine. I wouldn't be caught dead talking to her."

"You never say anything nice about anybody."

"You're just a country hick. You're as dumb as a doornail. You wouldn't even know about lipstick and perfume if I didn't tell you."

I changed desks the next day so that the boy who liked to put tacks on people's chairs and pull hair was behind Nora instead of me.

I had chicken pox. Dr. Lowe had quarantined me. I was in my room upstairs, my room with bare walls and bare windows and no heat and the February cold sneaking through the walls and the Jack-Frosted windows. No one was allowed to talk to me for fourteen days. They could bring my food and leave it at the head of the stairs and come and get the empty plates, but they couldn't come in and talk to me. When I was delirious, when I was itchy, when I had fever, when I was lonely, when I was bored, I had to stay alone. I was alone for a whole five days. I missed everybody.

"Sugah—" I heard the voice first. "People this side of the world so stupid, it's a mercy they still livin'. Why didn't you send Mr. Roitman to tell me you-all sick?" She sat herself on the edge of the bed and put her hand on my forehead. "Leavin' a poor little girl up here all alone."

"I'm not a little girl."

"Child, there's a little girl in every one of us till our dyin' day, and it's nothin' to be ashamed of."

From then on, my breakfast, dinner, and supper were brought right to my lap, and while I stuck my arm out from under the horsehide blanket to eat, she perched on my bed in her big coat, and told me jokes and stories—being "whupped" by her granny for talking like any little black pickanini, being a nurse in the war in England and getting a citation for nursing the black soldiers . . .

"What's wrong with black people?" I asked.

"I don't know, sugah. Nobody ever been able to tell me. I loved my black nanny more than I ever loved anybody. I been plenty places, and red, white, black, or blue, Catholic, Baptist, heathen, or Jew—put me blind in the middle of them, and I

42

wouldn't be able to tell the difference. Every blessed one of us just a mix-up of some bad and some good."

Papa came once. As soon as I saw his head above the stairs, I cried. He held me, and I cried and cried and cried.

"Do you want to go walking after school?"

It was Nora from behind me. The girl who usually sat there was at home with the chicken pox.

We walked out along the railroad tracks, past the yellow and white and green and orange elevators, past the dead slough covered with white snow.

"I got my monthlies," she said, huddling into the collar of her coat. Her eyes were grey now. Winter grey. Eaton's-sweater grey.

"So?" I said. "It's natural."

"Now I can have babies."

"No, you can't. You have to be married."

"I'm not ever going to get married." She started to cry. "I don't ever want anybody to do that to me. Would you want someone to do that to you? Right next to you all over? As tight as water?"

"But married people like it."

"No, they don't. Nobody likes it." And she cried harder. I didn't know what to say, so I put my arms around her and held her. She cried for a long, long time.

The next day, I told Janine about Nora crying.

"Don't married people like it?" I asked. "Mama says sex is for two people who love each other."

"I declare! Surely, they do. It's a way of sayin' 'I love you,' and sayin' it with your body and heart and mind. It's as natural as walkin' in the sun."

"But Nora doesn't want to have babies."

"Livin's about life, sugah. There's nothin' more important or excitin' than bringin' life into the world. And . . . think of it. All of us swimmin' in the same old pond of life. The birds and the bees and the flowers and the trees, kings and queens and little old you and me. All of us livin' and breathin' and wantin' and needin' and doin' the same things. Not one of us more important than the other. You go tell your Nora that."

I told Nora. But I lied about who told me.

"I don't care," she said. "I'm going to run away. I'm going to be a Chautauqua girl, and you can come."

"Why?"

"You can play the piano, and I can sing. We can go everywhere and do what we want and—"

"I don't want to run away."

"You're a chicken!"

"I am not! I roll my stockings and put on lipstick as much as you do."

"I bet you've never kissed a man."

"Neither have you."

"That's all you know."

"But what if you have a baby?"

"That's not how you have a baby." And she laughed and laughed and laughed.

I slapped her.

I ran home.

That night, I had a dream about when I was twelve and got my monthlies, and I thought I was dying, and Mama laughed. "It's natural, Sara." In my dream, she was still laughing. Then it was Nora in my dream laughing. Then—not laughing. Crying. Standing in the snow crying, all alone under a timid crescent moon, alone and crying. I woke up. I was crying, too.

I got out of bed and went to the window to look for the moon. I scraped a hole in the Jack-Frost forest. It was the shy moon of my dream. And another one on the snow. An orange glow across the snow, orange silk dancing on the blue-night snow.

Fire. The Jensen farm. Fire on Nora's farm.

I ran downstairs to the Roitman's room.

"Fire," I said. "Nora's farm is on fire."

In no time at all, it seemed, we were standing at the telephone in the hotel, and Mr. Roitman was ringing the emergency ring, ten rings, ten long rings, and telling everybody the farm, Nora's farm, was on fire. And then we were at the dray to get Mr. Roitman's horse and cutter. Dr. Lowe was there, and Billy Frank, and the Weyburn Security Bank manager. Mr. Roitman tried to make me go back. He said it was no place for me. But I wouldn't. And then we were sliding across the snow, cutters from town, from the other farms, laying ribbons toward the orange silk dancing against the night.

Nora's father was standing on the snow in shirtsleeves and overalls and no shoes, standing with a hunting rifle in his hand like he was on his way to get a pesky weasel, standing with the orange silk behind him, standing before our half-moon of wagons and cutters. Nora was lying on the snow, naked and still on the blue-night snow. A small white-cream body with a lipstick wound in her white-cream belly. There was no sound but the rustle and snap of the silk.

He stood there, holding his rifle, and he looked at her, and he looked at us, and his eyes were as dead as the slough. "She was an agent of the devil," he said. "I tried to wrestle it out of her. Every night, pretty near. And then the devil's child in her belly. I tried—"

He stopped. And he backed away from us, backed away from Nora, and turned and walked into the folds of the orange silk flames, and the orange flames danced higher.

I wouldn't go back to school, or Alkali Flats. I wouldn't go to the places Nora still was—in the empty desk, on the sidewalk on the way to Billy Frank's, in the snow crying under a thin silver moon.

When the Chautauqua came to Alkali Flats that summer, I didn't want to go. Mama said I had been feeling sorry for myself long enough, and if everybody laid down and died at the first bad thing that happened, where would the world be? It would do me good, she said.

The first thing I did when we got to town was to go see Janine. Two travellers, roundish and rumpled, were on the verandah.

"She's pretty good," one was saying.

"Janine? Are you kidding?" the other one said. "I had her last week, and she was terrible."

"Guess she didn't like your style," the first one said.

"She gets paid to like me," the second one said.

The first one turned to me. "I like you pretty good."

"Go on," the second one said to me. "Get out of here."

I went in to Janine. She was getting ready for the rush of people who would be there for the Chautauqua.

45

"I declare!" she said.

"Well, if everybody laid down and died at the first thing that happened, where would the world be?" I said.

"Amen," she said.

Then I told her what the travellers had said about her cooking.

"Cookin'?" she said.

She laughed, but the green sunrise light had gone out of her eyes.

"I don't think I'm in love any more," I said. "You can't be in love when people are dead."

"Sugah, one day you'll wake up and you'll know you got all kinds of room to feel all kinds of ways all at the same time."

The Chautauqua wasn't good for me.

The first night was a vaudeville show with two men who told stories and jokes about farmers and tripped each other, and two women, one fair and one dark. Like Nora and me. Fair and dark. The fair one, all pretty and sweet and blond and blue-eyed in a blue gown and with a blue parasol in her hand sang "Little Alice Blue Gown." Then came the dark one with her black hair and white skin in a glittering black beaded dress singing "Just the Kind of Girl Men Forget." And my mother, my very own mother, turned to Tsippa and me—"Let that be a lesson to you, girls." Tsippa, with her red-gold hair, looked right at me. Just as Little Alice Blue Gown waltzed across the stage with a man on each arm. And left the Girl Men Forget, that girl with black hair and white skin like mine, left her all by herself.

The show the second night was a man with flowing white hair and a white beard and a white suit—just like Mark Twain, Janine said—who talked for an hour about how in ten years the oil sources would dry out, and there would be no oil left anywhere in the world. Papa said it didn't matter, we'd gotten along without cars before, but Mama said what about trains? Where would the West be without trains? I couldn't sleep that night.

The third night, just before the show started and people were still getting the little kids to sit still on their laps, Bruce walked into the tent. That night was the best show of all. There was a mountain with real smoke coming out of it, and palm

46

trees, and beautiful brown people in grass skirts swaying like the willows, singing like the summer winds, singing and swaying for us, come thousands of miles from Hawaii to sing and dance for us. Bruce passed me after the show and winked.

When Mr. Roitman announced a party at his hotel for everybody, I wanted to go. I wanted to go almost more than I had ever wanted to do anything. I could hear the Alkali Flats Citizens' Band playing "Five Foot Two Eyes of Blue," all the way from the hotel, and I could hardly wait. I wanted to see them, the fair one and the dark one: I wanted to see them as close as my hand, as close and as clearly as glittering snowflakes, more intricate and more beautiful the closer you got to them. I wanted to dance. I wasn't too young any more. I wanted to dance with Bruce.

But when I found them—the blond one, grey and old and drunk already at the bar; the dark one, old, too, and knitting in the corner; the Mark Twain one saying his speech all over again—they weren't like snowflakes in your hand at all. They were like the jewel-blue water of the slough under a summer sky, and when you got close to it, put your hand in it, it was greenish water with mud on the bottom.

Then I saw Bruce. He was dancing with one of the beautiful brown women, holding her tight. Tight as water. One of the brown men went over and grabbed her by the arm.

Then Bruce was walking toward me, winking, holding his hand out to me, and we were on the dancefloor, and he was holding me. Tight. Tight as water. Tight as water and hot whiskey breath against my cheek. I remembered Nora huddled into her coat and crying, standing naked under a thin moon and crying.

I pulled away from him.

"Come on. Hey, come on!"

I ran. I ran out of the hotel, onto the verandah, down the street. He was right behind me, reaching for me. "Bitch. Bitch!"

"Here now, you-all." It was a strong, soft voice.

Bruce stopped.

"Whore," he said. "Both whores."

Janine walked toward me in the moonlight and put her arm around me, and we were sitting on the steps of Billy Frank's post office, and I was crying, and Bruce was gone, and the moon was watching.

And then Nora was gone. Really gone. Not huddling in her coat crying, not walking with me beside the dead slough, not painting me a lipstick mouth, not lying naked and still on the snow. I was glad. I was glad she could never know, never know that there had been nothing to run away to. Nothing at all.

6

Growing Pains

The sky was blue, and fluffy white clouds were pinned on it like butterflies on a bulletin board—and I was sitting on the steps of the verandah looking at my feet. I'd gone back to Alkali Flats for grade nine: now it was over, I'd been home for three hours, and there was nothing to do.

"Hey there, Little Flower!"

I looked up, following long skinny legs to a wide grin and wide honey-brown eyes under floppy honey-brown hair. It was Meyer. His family had come from New York the summer before: he had had a crush on me from the moment he laid eyes on me. He was holding a bright shiny saxaphone with wild roses in its mouth.

"Where'd you get that?"

"From the land of milk and honey, the land of *bagela* and *madela*." He handed me the roses. "Winnipeg. Swing time. Rag time. I just got back. Wanna' play, baby? You'n me, baby. We's music. Opening at the Alkali Flats Community Hall in three weeks. We're going to play at the dedication of no-name town, too."

"No-name town?"

"Our town. The one just over the hill where all that building is going on."

"You're crazy!"

"Feast your eyes, baby." He reached down, raised his pant leg, plucked out sheets of music tucked into his sock. " 'The Black Bottom,' 'Barney Google with the Goo-Goo-Googley Eyes,' 'Music Makes the World Go Round,' . . . and this—guess what this is?" He dangled a last sheet of music in front of my nose. "'Toot Toot Tootsie Good-bye.'"

"So?"

"So it's from 'The Jazz Singer.'"

"So?"

"So Al Jolson sings it, and he's a nice Jewish boy just like me. M-a-a-ammy how I love you, how I love you, my dear old—Come on. Let's go in and practise."

And in no time flat, everybody had crawled out of the woodwork and was standing around the piano watching us: Tsippa and the four cousins she had been so busy with only two minutes before; Gloomy Gertie and Mama Cow-Eyes Glanzman . . . The four cousins had come from Russia and were living with Aunt Sophie and Uncle Yacov. Gloomy Gertie and Mama Glanzman and Papa Glanzman and Dour Dave had come from Poland and were staying with us until their homestead was ready. They had already been at our place for a month, and Tsippa said Mama Cow-Eyes had been wearing a bottle-green, low-cleavage lounging robe and bright red lipstick the whole time. Mama Cow-Eyes was smiling at Meyer.

"Oh, brother," I said.

"*On gest prsystogny,*" Mrs. Glanzman said to Gloomy Gertie in Polish. "*Co on nim myslisz?*"

"Oh, oh," Meyer muttered.

"What did she say?"

"She said I was handsome."

Then Ulla was standing at the door, too. She was in a blue and white gingham dress, and she was pink and happy.

"Ulla," I said. "Did Carl ask you to marry him?"

She blushed.

"Why?"

"Because you're glowing. Mama says when a woman is in love, she glows."

She glowed a deeper pink. They had been going to dances together all winter, and everybody kept asking when they were going to get married. But he hadn't asked her yet.

"*Dus is bourgeois,*" one of the cousins said darkly. "*Der institution fon chassina is decadent.*"

"What did she say?" Ulla asked.

"She said, 'The institution of marriage is decadent,' in Yiddish. What are you doing here, Tsippa? I thought you were busy."

"Let's take five," Meyer said.

"What?" I said.

"That's Winnipeg jazz talk for 'I think we need a break.'"

We decided to walk over to Cactus Hill. Ulla talked about Carl all the way. "Don't you think he's good-looking? Imagine—he's so tall, and nice, and he likes me. Aren't I lucky? He comes over every night after he's finished for the day at the Wilkinson's, and then he helps Papa . . . Maybe we'll get engaged the day of the dedication. Then we could make an announcement. Wouldn't that be exciting?"

"Well—" I said.

"Yes," Meyer said warmly. "It would be." He poked me with his elbow. "What's wrong with you?"

"Nothing," I said. "Except that when Carl first came, Ulla couldn't stand him because he always got into fights."

"He doesn't any more," she said. Then—'Oh, look!"

We had reached the rise of Cactus Hill overlooking the new townsite. The tracks were being laid across the bottom of the hill, tracing the line of the coulee from east to west, a frame for the new town which would be set on the hill below us on a square against it. By next year, an elevator would be the northeastern point of the square, and a train station the southwestern point. On the north side of the tracks, the white canvas tents for the construction crew were giant mushrooms on the grey-green prairie wool. Between us and the slowly stretching railroad tracks, the foundation was being poured for Aunt Sophie's store. On the crest of Cactus Hill, string had been stretched around wooden pegs to mark where the basement would be dug for the new school. But that wasn't what Ulla was looking at. Prickly pear cactuses—large clear yellow blossoms, sunshine splashed on the earth—covered the hill.

They bloomed only once a year for one or two days, and always on June 30 and July 1. The hill was covered with them.

"What do you think they'll call the school?" Ulla said.

"The same as the town, whatever that is," Meyer said. "Nobody has any imagination."

"Papa wants the town to be called after Sara's father and Uncle Yacov," Ulla said.

"Gee," I said. "Imagine having a town named after you. It would be like being a king."

"Oh, no," Meyer said. "Now she thinks she's a princess."

A few days later, Meyer was back to practise again, and before we had finished our first run-through of "Shall I Have It Bobbed or Shingled," the four-year-old twins were standing on either side of me with shining eyes, Gloomy Gertie was perched on Papa's over-stuffed chair, and Mama Cow-Eyes Glanzman was standing at the door in that bottle-green robe holding a cigarette to her painted lips and smiling at Meyer.

"There's old Sara," Tsippa said as she trooped in the door behind her cousins, "showing off again."

"If you don't get out of here," I said, "I'll slit your throat."

"Take five," Meyer said. "We'll row out to the middle of the slough and play for the muskrats. You'll be safe there."

The sun was setting, and the long-legged avocets, bits of pink sunset trapped in their breast feathers, were stepping with careful elegance into their own reflections on the blue water. Two fawns were standing at the water's edge, wide-legged and surprised by a curious baby muskrat. Mama muskrat rolled on her back and chewed a juicy young cattail. It was almost dark when we rowed back to shore. Meyer hadn't played a note. God, he said, did it better.

Mama was standing at the door when we got back to the house. The twins were standing in their yellow-flowered nightgowns behind her.

"Where have you been?" she snapped.

"Rowing on the slough."

"Alone?"

"No. With Meyer. We went to practise."

"You're barely sixteen. He's twenty-two. If you want to practise, practise in the house. If you're not careful, you'll turn out like that woman upstairs doing nothing all day with her painted face."

One of the twins started to cry.

Mama glared at me. "Now see what you've done!"

I went out to find Papa. He was showing Mr. Glanzman and Dour Dave how to milk cows. Milking was women's work, but Papa didn't trust women to do it.

"What's wrong with Mama?" I asked. "She's acting funny."

He raised an eyebrow and shrugged.

I had my first kiss. Lips touching lips. It wasn't much. Not at first. It was right at our piano in our living room, too, not out in the pasture. After that, Meyer started stealing kisses. When he held me tight against him, tight as water, it wasn't awful at all.

Ulla came over. She was pale as death.

"What's wrong?"

"Carl," she said. "And Britt. She says he asked her to go with him to the dance at Westby."

"That's two-timing," I said.

"He'll probably buy her box instead of mine at the box social when we have the dedication. And after everybody thinking we're going to get married. I'll die."

"He wouldn't do that if he was nice. Neither would she. They should be boiled in oil. Both of them."

"How can you say that about him? I love him."

"We're too young to be in love."

"I'm not. I think about him all the time. I just have to see him coming down the road and my stomach gets into a knot. It's awful."

"Gee," I said. "Meyer just makes me laugh."

"Then you're not in love. It isn't supposed to make you happy all the time. You're supposed to go from the pinnacle of delight to the depths of despair at the shadow of a glance. I do."

I was sitting on the verandah looking through the catalogue. Meyer and I hadn't been practising as much because he was helping to get Aunt Sophie's store and the school ready

53

in time for the dedication in August. Then I heard his saxophone weaving a song into evening, threading its way through the clear-water song of the meadowlarks, the low notes of the cows, the bell-like laughter of the twins.

"Hey there, Little Flower, whatcha' doin'?"

"Picking out material to sew for grade eleven. And crochet thread for a sweater, in case the crop is good and Papa can afford to send me."

"You don't need to go to school. You're too smart already."

"I have to. I'm going to take piano lessons in Estevan and get my registered music teacher's certificate."

"What about the band of Meyer and Sara?"

I shrugged. "Papa wants me to."

"What about me?"

"What do you care?"

"What do I care! What do I care? I think I'll go drown in the slough. I think I'll get gored by the bull."

"Meyer!"

He was gone.

He didn't come back, either. When Tsippa and the cousins wanted to dance, there was only me to play.

"How come Meyer doesn't come any more?" Tsippa asked.

"Because he's helping with your mother's store, that's why."

"He only wants you for your dowry, anyway. Everybody thinks the Schillers are rich because we have a big farm. That's how they marry off girls who are stupid and ugly."

I hated her. I hated Meyer, too.

When I told Ulla, she said, "Don't you feel like killing yourself?"

Mama was in such a bad mood all the time that one day Papa decided we would leave the Glanzmans at home and go for a drive. Mama hadn't seen the town since the railroad crew had come, and now the mushroom tents were gone, leaving two gleaming bands of steel behind them. The basement was being dug for the school, and prickly pear cactuses were lying in lumps in the dirt. The walls for the first floor of Aunt Sophie's store were up, and the frame for their apartment on the second floor was being erected.

"Papa, don't you hate it that Uncle Yacov is moving from the farm?" I asked.

"Sara—" Mama said.

"Yes," Papa said. "I do."

"You'll still be partners, Aaron," Mama said.

"I'll run the farm. Yacov will run the machinery business. It's not the same. We won't be running the farm together."

Then the twins made up a silly name, Lumps of Dirt Dumb School, and everybody groaned and forgot about Uncle Yacov moving.

As soon as we got to Alkali Flats, Papa went to do some business at the Alkali Flats Telephone Company, and Saul took the twins to Billy Frank's to get the mail and their ice-cream cones.

"Now," Mama turned to me. She took a deep breath. "Come with me to the barber's."

"The barber's? What for?"

"What do you think?" She was nervous. "I have a surprise for your father."

She sat in the barber's red chair and unpinned her hair, rich black hair with red lights in it down to her waist. The barber held it in his hand. "Maybe," he said, "I cut only a little so it should be only a little surprise."

"No," she said. "All of it. Buster Brown."

"*Oy ve is meir,*" he said.

He cut it, and it lay in rich dark coils at his feet. It was part of my mother at his feet. I felt like crying. But Mama's blue eyes sparkled, and her cheeks were pink, and the short swingy Buster Brown cut framed her small face, and she looked sixteen.

"*Oy ve is meir,*" the barber said again.

Then we went visiting. Janine said, "Why, bless my soul!" and Mrs. Roitman said, "*Mein Gotte,*" and Mrs. Lowe said, "Eva!" By the time Papa came along with a chattering twin on each hand, we were waiting at the car. He stopped short. Mama smiled a pretty, shy smile. Papa looked confused. He kept looking at her funny all the way home.

"Hey, Little Flower!"

It was Meyer with a saxophone under his arm. And no roses.

"How come you're talking to me?" I asked.

"Because I forgive you for being so young and unfeeling. You are a victim of your youth."

"Gee," I said. "Really?"

By the night of our opening at the Alkali Flats Community Hall, Meyer and I knew twenty songs, enough to play different waltzes and fox trots and Charlestons for an hour and a half and then start over again. Except for the younger cousins ("*Dus is decadent*"), all of us kids from the farm were going, even Gloomy Gertie and Dour Dave who still didn't speak a word of either Yiddish or English.

Meyer and I were on the stage playing when Ulla and Carl came in. She was glowing again. Gloomy Gertie even had a kind of gloomy glow. The son of one of the Polish settlers was dancing with her. There were no Polish daughters. Dour Dave was leaning on the edge of the stage smiling at me.

It was right in the middle of a Charleston that I heard Mr. Dahl's voice. He was mad.

"By yumpin', those boys have done a lot around here. Who else should we name it for?"

"By heaven, if I'll go to a town with a Jew name!"

It was Mr. Wilkinson with that English accent he was so proud of.

I banged the lid down over the keys.

"Hey!" Meyer said.

"I don't feel like playing. Not for people like them."

"He's only one. People are staring."

"I don't care. One bad apple spoils the barrel."

"It's a big barrel," he said. "You can't even see him in it."

We took five.

When I got home, I woke Papa up. "If Mr. Wilkinson wouldn't come to a town with a Jew name, why was he coming to a dance where two Jews were playing?"

"Ssh. You'll wake Mama."

We went out to sit on the verandah.

"Listen," he said. "The world is singing."

The world *was* singing, singing silver shadows, and rustling leaves, and emerald and sapphire starlight.

"Mr. Wilkinson thinks he's better than everybody," I said.

"I'm not sure he does," Papa said. "Making other people

56

feel small is probably just his way of making himself feel big. Anyone who would go to all the trouble of acquiring an upper-class accent to cover up the fact that he escaped the slums of England . . ."

"I thought you said this was a new country."

"I'm afraid," Papa said, "people take their old ideas with them wherever they go. Don't ever get the idea that people like Wilkinson only pick on Jews, though. They're more dangerous than that. Remember Mr. Lin on the CPR construction crew? He was brought in to work, but he has to leave his family in China. And what about the boat load of people from India who weren't even allowed to set foot on shore? They were British subjects, and we turned them away because they were brown British subjects. Even if they had been allowed to land and live here, they wouldn't be full citizens. They couldn't vote. Neither can Mr. Lin. Neither can the Canadian Indians. Or your mother. Women can't vote, no matter what race they belong to."

"But Mr. Wilkinson never says anything nasty about anybody except Jews."

"It's popular right now because Hitler is making headway against us in Germany, and it looks like he can get away with it. But wait. Wait until Mr. Lin opens his cafe here. It won't be 'Mr. Lin.' It will be 'the Chinaman.' Except—" he glared at me in the pink light of dawn—"to my children. Do you under-stand?"

It was a cosy grey day with a comfortable grey rain. I was in the living room practising, and Ulla and Tsippa and the cousins had come over to dance. The older cousins and the twins were learning the Charleston and the Black Bottom. The younger cousins were waiting for me to play revolutionary dances.

Suddenly, Mama appeared in the doorway, her arms filled with crepe paper, left-over bits of cloth and ribbon, and boxes—hat boxes, shoe boxes, oatmeal boxes. . . . We were each to decorate one for the box social. On the day of the social, we would pack a lunch for two, and our "admirers" would bid on them to buy us and our lunch for the afternoon. The money would go to build a community hall.

"Not me," I said.

"*Dus is bourgeois*," the younger cousins said.

"Why not you?" Mama asked me. "Meyer will be looking for your box."

"No, he won't. I'm too young."

"Don't be smart, young lady."

"He just wants her for her dowry," Tsippa said.

"Don't be silly," Mama said. "There are no dowries in this country."

"*Dus is bourgeois*," the cousins said again.

"It's human nature," Mama said. "And it's fun. You might have secret admirers, all of you."

"If they're secret," I said, "they won't know which box is ours."

"Oh," she said knowingly. "They find out. Although your father didn't once. We were married, too."

"I bet you were mad," Tsippa said. "I bet you had a fight."

"Of course we did," Mama said. "What kind of man wouldn't know which box was his wife's?"

"Who will admire us?" the twins asked.

"Everybody," Mama said.

My box became a barn, red with a green roof and a black door at each end, like the barn on our farm. Ulla's box became the Union Jack, a proud bold flag in red, white, and blue. The twins made twin boxcars. There was wheat inside, they said. Mama's was a doll with blue button-eyes and woolly brown hair. Mrs. Glanzman's was red with a red paper flower. So was Gloomy Gertie's. Tsippa's was green with a red flower. The older cousins pasted patches of lace and ribbon on white boxes to make wedding blouses. The younger cousins flounced out in disgust.

"Everything is *bourgeois unt decadent*," I said. "Don't they ever have any fun?"

"Now, Sara," Mama said. "Have some patience. They've only been here a few months."

"You think life is just crocheting blouses and playing at dances," one of the older cousins sneered. "How would you like to see your mother raped and shot? How would you like to see your father and brothers sent to Siberia? How would you like to spend months in the forests in the winter hiding from the Cossacks?"

58

"Then how come you're not revolutionary like your younger sisters?"

"What makes you think we're not?"

I pointed at their wedding-blouse boxes. "'*Dus is bourgeois,*' remember? If your know-it-all sisters are real revolutionaries, they're going to have to fight for justice for everybody. Are they going to fight for people from India, and the Chinese, and the Canadian Indians? When you fight for others, you fight for yourself. No one stops with just Jews or just Indians."

"Good heavens, Sara," Mama said. "Where did you get all that?"

"Oh, no place," I said. "But I'm right, aren't I?"

"Yes," she said. She looked at me as if she had never seen me before. "You are."

Meyer and I were practising in the living room, and Mr. Dahl and Papa were on the verandah arguing.

"There are only a few weeks before the dedication," Mr. Dahl growled. "We have to decide on a name for the town sometime."

"I hear some of the other boys have been talking," Papa said. "It could mean trouble."

"By yumpin', why should you let people like Chicken George and Wilkinson—"

"Thor," Papa said. He was upset. "It's not worth it. What matters for Yacov and me is that from now on it will only be a short haul to take a load of grain in to the elevator. That's what we've all worked for, isn't it?"

Meyer was stealing a kiss. I didn't want to let him because men shouldn't want women for dowries. Just then, Gloomy Gertie came in. "*Ona go caluge!*" she shrieked. "*Ona go caluge w obecnosci innych!*" And she went out to Papa and Mr. Dahl and screeched a lot of other things in Polish. Then she hot-footed it to Mama Cow-Eyes sitting and smoking in the kitchen, and Mama Cow-Eyes hot-footed it over to Aunt Sophie's, and Aunt Sophie screamed at Uncle Yacov, and Uncle Yacov went to Papa, and Papa questioned me, and Mama exploded.

"A kiss on the piano bench! She's a fine one to talk! Her,

bending over you every day, showing everything she's got. In front of me! In front of her own son and daughter!"

"Who?" Papa asked, completely bewildered. "Who?"

"That . . . that maid! Steals women's husbands. In my own house!"

"What are you talking about?"

"How do you think she got Mr. Glanzman? She was their maid. He left his own wife and children for . . . for that! And what do you think they're doing here? They're starting over where nobody knows them. She told Sophie herself. She's proud of it. She never lifts a finger, she sits all day in my kitchen with her painted face and her cigarette— and I never even have time to wash my face!" And she burst into tears.

Papa didn't say anything. He just put his arms around her and kissed her on the tip of her ear. Then he went out to Mr. Glanzman, and Mr. Glanzman came in to talk to Mama Cow-Eyes upstairs, and Mama Cow-Eyes came steaming downstairs with as many of her clothes as she could carry, and picked her way across the yard among the horse buns to Aunt Sophie's. The next day, the whole Glanzman family left. Uncle Yacov drove them to the Alkali Flats train station, and they went to stay at the Isreals' boardinghouse where the little red bitey bed-bugs lived. And Mama sang and made up bedtime stories for the twins for the first time all summer.

"Sara," Papa said at breakfast one morning. "You're in charge of finding a name for the school. We decided at the school-board meeting last night that it's up to you kids."

So we had a meeting. Tsippa said we should walk over and look at the school so we would be inspired. When we got there, we had a fight. The revolutionary cousins said there was no choice. It was being built by the people of south Saskatchewan for the people of south Saskatchewan, so it was the South Saskatchewan People's School. Ulla said it was on Cactus Hill, and it should have a name as pretty as where it was. Tsippa said Ulla wouldn't be going to it, anyway, and Ulla said her children would be. Then the revolutionary cousins said a name should mean something, and the twins started to cry and said school meant school, like Mama meant Mama. Saul said the twins were right. Then Tsippa said it should be named after the town, and

I said she had no imagination, and she flounced off with her four cousins trailing behind her.

After everyone had left, Ulla told me that Carl had told her that he loved both her and Britt, and I told her that Carl and Britt deserved each other, and she left, too.

"For heaven's sake," Mama said, "the whole thing is ridiculous. Why don't you just pull the names out of a hat?"

The morning of the dedication was cool, late August cool with a nip of fall in the night and the warming summer sun in the day. By noon, everyone was there, people from across the line, Estevan, and even Regina. They were all talking about the name for the school and for the town because all the local residents had to put the names they'd chosen into one of the hats the twins were carrying.

Uncle Yacov climbed onto a sawhorse table and held aloft a box hat with coneflowers and brown-eyed susans set prettily in the brim.

"I'll start off the bidding myself," he said. "And I dare anyone to bid against me."

"Fifteen dollars," Mr. Dahl said.

"Sixteen," Dr. Lowe said.

"I thought you boys were my friends," Uncle Yacov said. "This is my wife's, and no one's eating my wife's cooking but me. Bidding closed. Twenty dollars."

"What if Carl buys Britt's box and doesn't buy mine?" Ulla asked.

"Then you can get rid of him because you're too good for him."

"Are you afraid Meyer won't buy your box?" she asked.

"I don't care."

I didn't know the next box. I went to put my name into the hat for the school. Hillcrest.

"Oh, no," Ulla groaned.

It was Britt's box. Carl had just bought Britt's box. For $6.50. Britt was triumphant. Not glowy, like Ulla was when she was with Carl. Triumphant. I thought Ulla was going to cry. But, instead, her eyes flashed cobalt blue.

"To hell with him!"

"Ulla!" Mrs. Dahl said.

61

"By yumpin'!" Mr. Dahl said.

"Just wait," Ulla said. She went up to the front and picked out her own box and handed it to Uncle Yacov.

He held it up.

"What am I offered for the Union Jack?" he began.

"Five dollars," Carl said.

"Ten," Ulla shouted.

Suddenly, it was very quiet.

"Ten," Uncle Yacov said. "Do I hear—"

"Fifteen," Ulla said.

"Sold," Uncle Yacov said.

"Thank you, sir," Ulla said sweetly.

It was Mrs. Dahl's box next, wrapped in blue and white gingham.

"Fifty dollars," Mr. Dahl said.

"Fifty dolla . . ." Uncle Yacov said. "Thor!"

"Never mind. I work my share. I have two strong arms, worth more than fifty dollars."

Next was a box decorated like a barn, red with a green roof.

"Well," Uncle Yacov said. "Must be a very sensible farm girl who made this. A good farmer's wife."

"Twenty-five cents."

It was Meyer.

Uncle Yacov almost dropped it. "Twenty-five cents? You want to win your lady's love with twenty-five cents?"

"Twenty-five dollars."

I looked for the voice. It wasn't Meyer.

"That's better. Twenty-five dollars. Do I hear—"

It was over. Dour Dave had bought me for the afternoon. The knots in my stomach tightened.

"I guess the Isreals' brought him all the way from Estevan just for you," Tsippa said sweetly. "I didn't think he knew that much English."

Meyer came over to hiss at me.

"Some little flower! A Venus flytrap. He knew it was your box, didn't he? Protecting little Sara. How much money does he think I have?"

"How would Uncle Yacov know it was mine? He's just trying to raise money for the community hall."

He stomped off, and as I watched him walk away, the knots

tightened. I had made honey cake for Meyer, and Dour Dave was going to eat it.

The rest of the afternoon was mixed up with my knots. I remember Dr. Lowe getting up on the sawhorse table afterwards to speak to us like a parent because, he said, he had delivered most of us and had a right to, and our parents would probably never say it. They had worked hard for us, he said, and the only thing they asked was that we would do our share when the time came. Then the twins handed him their hats. He reached in, and out came the name for our school. Ulla's name. Cactus Hill.

When the name for our new town was read out, there was laughter all the way up to the top of the hill and back down again. Short Haul. When Mr. Dahl led a prayer in Norwegian, and Uncle Yacov in Yiddish, and Mr. Wilkinson in English, there were amens in many, many accents.

Except from Meyer, who didn't speak to me for the rest of the afternoon or evening. Not even to tell me which song we were playing next. Now, Ulla said, I was in love.

7

Jewish Girls

Goldie was standing at the door waiting for me. She had bubbly brown curls and the widest greenest prettiest eyes I had ever seen, and she was wearing a brown tweed skirt with a soft orange sweater. I looked at myself in the hall mirror. I was wearing the lemon-yellow Black Bottom sweater Meyer had given me before he stopped speaking to me and the taupe skirt I had made to go with it. I looked almost as good as her. I didn't look like I came from the country.

"Come on," Goldie said. "We'll be late. Paul has already gone."

"Who's Paul?"

"My brother."

"Oh."

Goldie had seven brothers and sisters.

"Is he the one in grade twelve?"

"Yeah."

We walked past neatly painted houses: white with green trim, white with red trim, yellow with white trim . . . Just beyond and below, on the bronze and copper folds of the valley, the bare trees were brown and black lines. Estevan

Collegiate, a big brick square building alone in the middle of a sandy yard, was a mile up the street.

"Come on, Sara," Goldie said. "You can sit behind me."

There was somebody sitting in that seat already, a very long stretched-out boy with harum-scarum sandy hair.

"You don't mind, do you, Sydney?" Goldie said. "You don't like sitting behind me, anyway."

"What makes you think I'm going to like sitting behind her?" he said, picking up his books and unwinding out of his seat. He looked down at me with disgust.

The bell rang.

"Quick," Goldie said. "It's the principal. He's really tough. He was in the war."

Mr. McMonigle walked into the room, ramrod straight. He surveyed us with steel-grey eyes. The eyes stopped at me.

"You must be Miss Schiller. We were expecting you at the beginning of September. Six weeks ago."

There was a snicker from the back of the room. The eyes moved on.

Mr. McMonigle taught Latin. I had never heard of Latin.

I'd never heard of the next subject, either. Composition. With Miss Prately. She was prim and plump, and we weren't going to "compose" at all; we spent the whole period de-composing sentences into subjects and predicates, into nouns and verbs and objects, into prepositions and articles and adverbs and adjectives. The next subject was Miss Prately's, too: literature. "Ugh," Goldie said. "She always makes us memorize." The recitations began at the front of the room with the mayor's daughter. It was Grey's "Elegy in a Country Churchyard."

"You might say," Miss Prately said in a weedy churchyard voice, "that we in Saskatchewan are the country churchyard—lonely and forgotten."

"Oh, brother," I said.

"Excuse me?" she said sharply.

I felt my cheeks burn. I hadn't meant to say it.

"It was Miss Schiller," Sydney said. "The new country girl."

"Do you," she said, turning in my direction, "wish to speak?"

I shook my head.

"We're waiting."

"It's just that . . . it's just that I don't feel like we're dead."

"Oh, well," she said. "You're young yet," and she nodded for the next recitation.

Suddenly, right in the middle of it—and it was the lawyer's daughter, too—there was a screech from Miss Prately. "Syd-ney!" She pointed to the wastepaper basket beside the classroom door.

Sydney was chewing.

"Syd-ney!" she screeched again, in exactly the same tones, an interval of a minor thirteenth.

Syd-ney! unwound out of his seat, still chewing, and clumped across the back of the room, up the side along the windows, to cross in front of Miss Prately to the wastepaper basket.

"Oh, brother," Goldie said.

After lunch, we had French. The teacher walked in and glared at us. "Miss LaVallee hates us," Goldie whispered. In biology class, I fainted. When I woke up, there was a circle of faces looking down on me, and prim, plump Miss Prately, the decomposing literature teacher, holding a wet lavender hanky to my forehead in a prim, plump fashion. That night, I had a dream that it was Miss LaVallee holding the hanky instead of Miss Prately, pressing hard on my forehead, hard like she was trying to squash me.

The next morning, Goldie was there again, and there was a dream man—tall, dark, and handsome with black hair and wide green eyes and long eyelashes—waiting behind her.

"Paul," Goldie said. "How come you're walking with us?"

"Because, Half-pint—"

"Don't call me that!"

"Because, Half-pint," he repeated, "we're going in the same direction, and because you're my sister, and because I love to be with you."

"Since when?"

A car honked behind us.

"Hey, Paul, what are you doing with the girls?" It was a boy from the car, good-looking, dark-haired, and sneering. There were two more in the car just like him.

"Yeah, Paul," Goldie said. "What are you doing with the girls?"

He got into the car. They drove off.

"How come they didn't ask us to go with them?" I asked.

"Are you kidding?" she said. "The Zeisman boys are worse than the Christian boys. They wouldn't be caught dead with a Jewish girl."

"He's really good-looking," I said.

"Who? My brother? Yeah. Just like me."

"You are," I said. "You're really pretty."

"Yeah," she said again. "Sure I am."

We had literature and composition again, and Syd-ney! did it again, in both classes; Miss Prately screeched in a minor thirteenth, and Syd-ney! clumped up to the wastepaper basket and kissed his gum good-bye. In biology class, as soon as the jar with the frogs was opened, I fainted again. Then we had Miss LaVallee, glaring, staring Miss LaVallee. By noon, I felt like crying.

"What's wrong?" Goldie asked.

"I'll never pass."

"Sure you will."

"No, I won't. I never took French or Latin or biology before."

"You didn't? How come?"

"Because in Alkali Flats we only had to write departmental exams for literature, history, geography, and arithmetic, so that's all we learned."

"Girls don't need all those other subjects, anyway. You can come with me to Winnipeg and be a secretary. Come on. Let's go up to the auditorium and dance. That'll cheer you up."

I followed her up to the third floor of the school. At the end of the auditorium under the basketball net, somebody— the doctor's daughter, Goldie said—was playing "Five Foot Two Eyes of Blue" on the piano. It was awful. One of the Zeisman boys was dancing with the mayor's daughter, and the other was dancing with the lawyer's daughter. The dream man wasn't dancing.

At one o'clock, the bell rang, and we trooped back down to our classes on the first floor.

"I thought you said it would cheer me up," I said.

"Why? Didn't it?"

"Nobody asked us to dance. Not even your brother."

"Nobody ever asks Jewish girls to dance. Not even the Jewish boys."

"Why not?"

She shrugged.

"Then why do you go up?" I asked.

"I don't care. I don't dance, anyway."

I went to my first music lesson feeling glowery.

The door to the little white house was opened by a little man with bristling white eyebrows and a bristly white beard and eyes that laughed so that you couldn't help but laugh with them. "Miss Sara Schiller, I presume," he said, shaking my hand vigorously. There was the music of Scotland in his voice. "I'm Mr. Rae. Of course, I'm no one but 'Scotty' since I set foot on the prairies. And yet this is the 'English School of Music,' for no one would trust the Scottish school, thinking we've nothing but bagpipes on the moors."

I was bustled through a neat little house and out the back. We crossed the yard to an old chicken coop overlooking the valley. The setting sun was a clear and burnished gold in the sharp October wind. The door to the chicken coop was opened, and we entered a music studio, music books lining the walls, a braided rug on the floor, a pot-bellied stove, and a piano with a globe sitting on it.

I played.

"Yes," he said. "Intermediate. And you want to get your music-teaching certificate, do you not? How long have you studied, then?"

"Three years at Mrs. Lowe's in Alkali Flats."

"Hmmm. Yes. Very good. To become a registered music teacher, however, you will have to work very hard. We shall see at the recital at the Orpheum Theatre in February."

"A recital?" I said.

"Yes. Yes, indeed," he said, bobbing his head.

I went to Goldie's to complain. It was easy to find Goldie's house, even if you had never been there before because they lived above their bakery: you followed the aroma of cinnamon and raisins down the street, and once you opened the door on the ground floor to the stairway upstairs, you followed the sound of a million kids scrapping to the second floor.

"Those are my stockings."

"That's a lie!"

"Where's my shirt?"

"How should I know?"

I knocked.

"Let me open it!"

"No, I want to!"

A little miniature dream man stood in the doorway with four more little dream boys and girls behind him. Goldie sent them downstairs to get cinnamon rolls. We had tea, and the little people sang and tap-danced, and I complained and Goldie made it worse: everybody went to the recital, she said, they went all dressed up and showing off. Then we talked about boys. I told her about Meyer liking me and not speaking to me any more, and she told me about staying with her aunt and uncle in Bromhead to help in their store, and meeting a boy who wasn't Jewish. His parents went crazy, and her aunt and uncle shipped her right back to Estevan. Now he wrote her secret letters. It was very romantic.

That night, I dreamed about the recital. The Orpheum Theatre was filled, and Sydney was chewing gum and snickering at the back, and the French teacher was sitting in the front row glaring. There was a jar of dead frogs on the top of the piano.

The next time we trooped up to the auditorium, the same wrong-note, no-rhythm girl was playing. "Oh, brother," I said to Goldie. "Not her again."

"I suppose you think you can do better?"

It was Sydney, chewing gum behind me.

"She sure can," Goldie said, pushing me to the front. "Go on, Sara. Show him."

"Hear ye, hear ye," Sydney said. "Schiller thinks she can do better. Country mouse comes to town. Come on, Myrtle, move over. Schiller thinks she can do better."

I did.

After that, almost every time we went up to dance in the auditorium, I had to play. But even on the days when I waited in the classroom pretending to finish something until I heard Miss Wrong Note playing, nobody danced with me. It was awful, just standing there, me and Goldie and the other Jewish girls and all the ugly girls, watching each time a boy walked across to our side of the auditorium, hoping he was going to ask us, afraid he wasn't going to ask us, watching as he asked somebody else.

At night, when I tried to study, my Latin verbs and the French verbs were all mixed up with Mr. McMonigle's steel-grey eyes, and Miss LaVallee's hate-eyes, and the headaches I had left over from fainting when the bottles with formaldehyde were opened.

And then Mr. McMonigle gave us a Latin test, and I was called into his office. The wind rattled the windows behind his head. The sky was a clear, cold blue.

"Well, Miss Schiller," he said. "You got 25 percent. Do you have anything to say?"

I didn't.

"What do you intend to do?"

I took a deep breath.

"If I don't do better by Christmas, I'll drop it."

He nodded. I left.

Paul was in the hall.

"What did he say?"

"Who?"

"The principal, Hayseed. That's his office, isn't it?"

I told him.

"Why didn't you tell him you only studied four subjects in grade nine and ten?"

I didn't know. I didn't know he knew. I didn't think it would make any difference, anyway.

"Well, at least," he said, "he'd know that it isn't just because you're dumb or lazy. I bet you didn't tell him you missed school because you had to help your mother with the harvest, either, did you?"

I hadn't.

Just then, Goldie came along.

"What are you doing here?" she asked her brother.

"What are you doing here?"

"Going to the bathroom."

"Great minds think alike. That's just what I'm doing, Half-pint."

I stayed after school to get an extra Latin assignment from Mr. McMonigle. As I was leaving the building, I felt something sprinkling on my head. It wasn't rain. It was sand. It was Paul raining sand on me.

"Hey!" I said.

"Hey, yourself, Hayseed. Staying in after school?"

"Sort of."

"Me, too. I helped clean up the chem lab. So, how's the big city treating you?"

"Not bad."

"You must be a farmer."

"I am. So what?"

"Don't get mad. It's what the farmers who come into the bakery say, that's all. Ask them anything—'Hear you got rusted out last week. How was it?' 'Not bad.' 'Hear there was a lot of rain out your way. How're the roads?' 'Not bad.' 'Hear you got hit by a train last night. How're you feeling?' 'Not bad.'"

I laughed.

"Well?"

"Well what?"

"How's the big city treating you?"

"Terrible," I said.

"How come?"

I shrugged.

"Just like a farmer. Come on."

He led me over the ochre grasses of the valley down to the creek bubbling liquid blue over the rocks.

"What are you going to be when you grow up?" Paul asked.

"A music teacher, I guess. What are you going to be?"

"A doctor."

"Gee," I said. "I'd be a doctor if I were a man. Zaida used to say that the highest thing a Jew could do was to save a life. You can break any of the religious laws if it will save a life."

"Yeah," Paul said. "Except for the Jewish quota at the medical school. You can't break that law." He threw a rock into the creek. It didn't disturb the bubbling and the gurgling at all. "Mama and Papa can't afford it, anyway. Bakeries don't make that much money."

71

We sat facing the warmth of a pale sun, listening to the dry copper leaves in the wind, and the whispers and sighing of the bronze grasses. We sat, part of the silence and the whispers, part of the gold and the copper and the bronze.

The world was becoming violet shadows when we climbed out of the valley. That night, as I did my Latin and French verbs, it wasn't the steel-grey or the hate-eyes I saw, but Paul's, wide and green, and the tease in them when he called me Hayseed.

Gold Rush was on at the Orpheum Theatre. Goldie and I were going. As we turned onto Main Street, a car slowed behind us, and we heard a long, low wolf-whistle. The car drew abreast, then speeded up, sputtering gravel behind it. A head in the back seat slid out of sight.

"Serves them right," Goldie said, laughing fit to kill.

"Who? Why?"

"The Ziesman boys and Paul. They didn't recognize us."

"How do you know?"

"Do you think my own brother would whistle at us if he knew it was us?"

They were going to the movie, too.

Everybody was there. Scotty was at the piano at the front, his white bristly beard bobbing over the keys as he played. There was Mr. McMonigle, still ramrod straight but gentler, somehow, away from the school, and smiling; scowly-owly Miss LaVallee; prim and plump Miss Prately with a prim and plump and proper little man; the mayor, rumpled and friendly and the mayor's wife, neat and unfriendly; the mayor's daughter and the doctor's daughter and the dentist's daughter and the lawyer's daughter . . . The daughters were together on the left side of the theatre. The boys were on the opposite side, laughing and hitting each other on the shoulder.

"Boys are so dumb," Goldie said. "Just think, you'll be sitting up there in front of everybody, just like Mr. Rae. The recital is always on a Friday, you know, so there's no movie, so everybody goes to the recital instead."

"Goldie," I said. "How many times do I have to ask you to stop reminding me? I'm trying to forget."

I had the dream again that night of playing in front of

everybody, and Sydney snickering, and the dead frogs on top of the piano.

There was a party at the Zeisman's for Mrs. Zeisman's cousin who was visiting from Winnipeg. There were always parties, Goldie said, for *brise*s and *bar mitzvah*s and anniversaries and for birthdays and for new settlers . . . Mrs. Zeisman liked to have everything at her place, Goldie said, so that she could show off her three-storey house and her stained-glass window and her jewel of a maid.

Goldie came to get me. I was wearing the yellow moire taffeta dress Mama had made me. It shimmered in the light. Goldie was in a pretty green dress that matched her eyes. Sometimes, she said, she let the dress go to parties by itself: it knew everyone as well as she did.

The jewel of a maid greeted us at the door and presented us to Mrs. Zeisman, a tiny barrel-shaped lady.

"Sarela! Goldela! Such *shene medela*s, such beautiful girls. I shouldn't be surprised you will both be married women soon. Come. Sarela, you will play for us, for my cousin. Who knows? Maybe there'll be something? Then you will have some tea. Girls like you shouldn't worry to diet. A man likes a woman not too skinny, he should have something to hold onto."

She plunked me down at the piano and left.

"Never mind her," Goldie said. "Let's go get something to eat. Mama brought knishes."

"Where's Paul?" I asked.

"Why? Who wants to know?"

"I was just wondering."

"Sarela." It was Mrs. Zeisman again. "You haven't played." Goldie disappeared.

The cousin was little and round like Mrs. Zeisman and stood at the piano and watched me with bright beady eyes until he was taken away to watch somebody else.

"You were flirting!"

It was Paul.

"I was not. And even if I was, what do you care? You never dance with me, anyway."

"Nobody's dancing. Do you see anybody dancing?"

"I'm talking about at school."

73

"Nobody dances with Jewish girls."

"Then I guess they don't have to talk to them, either."

Mrs. Zeisman came up to lead me back to the piano.

"And how is your mother, poor woman? What kind of life is it for her in the country? In the city, you have people to talk to, you can educate your children . . . Why should your father keep her in the country? Come. I'll show you the house. This rug. From Turkey. Mr. Zeisman came home, 'Ruchela, I have a surprise for you. Guess what it is!' How could I guess? Something so expensive, who could guess?"

She talked all the way up to the third floor and the stained-glass window and back down again, and when she turned into the dining room, I kept on walking, down the hall, through the door, and out. When Goldie asked me the next day what had happened to me, I said I had gotten a formaldehyde headache.

"Why, lass," Scotty said to me when I came in for my lesson that week, "you're looking as black in your soul as a Scottish loch in January. When the winter dark descends on my soul, I come to my globe, and close my eyes, and spin it, and put down my finger—and there I am, riding an elephant, or walking with a penguin. That's how I came to this part of the world, you know. I closed my eyes, and spun the globe, and followed my imagination."

"Are you sorry? Miss Prately says we're lost and forgotten, like the country churchyard."

"Ach—we all miss what we can't have, and many of us have imaginations that lively—we miss what we never had. To hear some of these fine folk talk, the sun always shone, and they were lords and ladies of the manor. Well, it's as sure as the heather in the spring that the lords and ladies don't give up life beside a warm fire to begin again with nothing but their bare hands to help them."

I spun the globe. When I opened my eyes, I was on an island in the Caribbean Sea.

"What would you be knowing about the West Indies, then?"

"Nothing."

"Ah. Then you won't be able to follow your letter quite so well."

"What letter?"

"The letter to the postmaster general asking for stamps."

We wrote a letter together, and he put a dollar in it for me, and a stamp on it, a 1927 twelve-cent stamp that was an 1898 map of the British Empire. On my way to the post office, in my mind's eye, I was on the train chugging across spring-green prairie under sun-pale skies, along sparkling azure lakes, and through perfumed pine forests. Then my mind's eye didn't know any more.

I had a dream that night. All of us, the whole school, were on the boat with my letter, and Miss LaVallee was holding a strap and marching us, even the Zeisman boys and Paul, in a circle. It was the boys who were laughing and calling her "Frenchie" and "half-breed," but she picked me out of the circle. I stumbled against her, and when I looked up, it wasn't Miss LaVallee any more, but my grade three teacher, with her arm raised to beat me.

The next day, going in to class, Miss LaVallee was there at the door, just like in the dream, with the same dream hate. I backed away from her, backed down the hall, backed away from the dream hate. I went into Mr. McMonigle's office. He looked up from his desk. The skies were wet-grey through the window behind him.

"Mr. McMonigle, I am dropping French."

He raised an eyebrow.

"I'm too far behind," I continued, "and it's holding me back in my other subjects."

He nodded. I left.

I went to the library for the rest of the period and looked in the encyclopedia. My letter would travel by train until Montreal, financial capital of Canada, and then it would get on a boat and sail down the mighty St. Lawrence River, gateway to North America, past bobbing seals and blowing white beluga whales, to spill into the Atlantic Ocean. My letter would pass rocky coasts and cliffs, sandy beaches and fishing villages, sailing down the Atlantic coast from grey-green northern waters to warm blue, from ice to sun. My letter was going to palm trees and aqua seas and sugar cane and rum.

75

When I looked out over the valley, a soft, peaceful snow was laying white satin lace over the copper and the bronze.

Mr. McMonigle was coming in to speak to our class about *The Merchant of Venice*. "But first, Syd-ney!" Miss Prately said in her interval-of-a-thirteenth voice and pointing to the wastepaper basket. "Na," Sydney said. And swallowed.

Mr. McMonigle strode in.

"Students, I want you to understand that this is a play, and it does not apply to people in general."

"You mean Jews," Sydney said from the back.

"What do you think, class?" Mr. McMonigle said, his steel-grey eyes on Sydney. (Sydney was looking at his feet.) "What do you think this play is about?"

"Money," Goldie said.

"Just like a Jew," Sydney said.

"Well, I think," I said, "Shylock's daughter should be boiled in oil. She's the real villain. Shylock was just doing his job."

"Excuse me?" Mr. McMonigle said. "She was the villain?"

My cheeks were burning. Even my ears were burning. I hadn't meant to say it.

"She broke one of the Ten Commandments—'Honour thy father and mother'—and she did it publicly, too. She rejected her own father, and she rejected his religion. How would all those Christians in the play who thought she was so wonderful have liked it if one of their daughters rejected Christianity and humiliated them in public? They'd have burned her at the stake."

"Dear me," Mr. McMonigle said.

"It's not fair. Nobody here knows what it's like for Jews in the old country. Mama says money-lending is one of the few occupations they're allowed. They have to make a living somehow, and no money lender is any better or worse than any other money lender. It's got nothing to do with their religion."

"I think you can carry on with the play, Miss Prately," Mr. McMonigle said.

I went home at lunchtime, and I had a migraine headache.

Goldie was at the station to meet me after Christmas

76

holidays, and we went to Krivel's cafe for a lemon soda.

"So? Are you glad to be back? Did Meyer talk to you?"

"He wasn't there. He went to Winnipeg. My cousin Tsippa says he went to look for a wife. But I don't have to go to Mrs. Zeisman's again if I don't want to, or any more parties, and Mama and Papa promised they'll come to the recital."

"I don't know why you worry about the recital so much. You play in front of the kids at school all the time. Everyone thinks you're great."

"Oh, sure. How come hardly anyone ever talks to me, then?"

"They don't talk to me, either."

The next morning, I was watching at the window for Goldie and feeling glowery.

But it wasn't Goldie coming up the walk. It was Paul. I opened the door.

"Goldie's sick. She said to tell you to go without her."

"Thank you."

I started to close the door.

"Aren't you going to school?"

"Of course."

"Come on, then. You'll be late."

"You've got a lot of nerve! You haven't even talked to me for two months!"

"You're not the only girl in Estevan."

"Do you go down to the creek with the mayor's daughter, too?"

"No."

"I bet. They only like cars."

"Oh, come on. I'm sorry."

"Thank you."

"Hurry up. Here comes one of the sleighs from the coal mine. If we run, we can jump on and get a ride to school."

The next morning, there he was, walking up the sidewalk and whistling. "Oh," I said in my best what-a-surprise voice. "What are you doing here?"

"Hurry up! I hear the sleighbells."

I hurried. I jumped. I missed.

"What kind of country girl are you?" Paul asked, pulling

77

me up out of the snow. The sleigh was gone. The snow was quiet and fluffy, like being awake inside your own dream. "How's the big city treating you?"

"Pretty good," I said. "And don't tell me I sound like a farmer."

"I won't. You do. What's wrong?"

I shrugged. He pushed me back into the snow.

He was there again the next day, and I didn't pretend to be surprised. When the sleigh came by, I didn't miss. But as I settled onto the coal-dust bed of the empty sleigh, Paul was no longer laughing. I followed his eyes to the driver, coal dust eating into the lines of his face, into the white pile of a ragged sheepskin jacket: a coal-dust etching against a winter-white sky.

We jumped out at the school and watched the sleigh draw away until it was only a black smudge against the white.

"It makes me mad!" Paul said.

"What does?"

"The miners. They don't even work for a wage. They only get paid for the weight of the coal they bring up from the mine, and the weighers cheat, so they don't even get what they should for that. And if they get caught buying anywhere except at the company stores, they get their pay docked."

"How do you know all that?"

"They come into the bakery sometimes, and we give them the day-old bread and rolls and doughnuts."

We went into the school. When Syd-ney! clumped up to the front of the room to spit out his gum, I snapped at him.

"Why don't you just swallow it, you dumb ox?"

"It's not good for me."

The next day, Paul and I let the sleigh pass.

"Hey!" It was Goldie.

"Hello, sis."

"You left without me."

"You weren't ready. Besides, I don't always walk with you."

"No, you sure don't."

"Two's company. Three's a crowd."

She didn't turn around to talk to me for the rest of the day. The next morning, when I answered the door, it was Goldie. Paul wasn't there.

"Paul went with the Zeisman boys," she said.

"Oh," I said.

"There's a movie about sex," she said. "Do you want to go? I bet you'd rather go with Paul."

"Are you kidding? Not to a movie about sex. Besides, we don't go places together. We just talk."

There was no one at the movie from school except Goldie and me. Not even the boys were there. And it wasn't about sex. It was about syphilis, about your hair falling out and sores all over your body and screaming in mental asylums. I felt like throwing up.

"It'll be a frosty Friday in June before I have a boyfriend again," Goldie said.

"Me, too."

I had a dream that night that Paul had kissed me, and my fingers were rotting. I was sitting at the piano on the stage at the Orpheum Theatre in front of everybody, and my fingers were rotting off in bits onto the keys. The next time Goldie was sick and Paul came to get me, I looked into his eyes, and they weren't his eyes, but the crazed, pained eyes of the movie, of the dream. When he touched me, I pulled back, pulled back from my dream.

"What's wrong?"

"Nothing."

"Are you mad at me?"

I shook my head.

"Are you homesick?"

I shook my head again.

"Come on. Cheer up. Did I ever tell you about the man from Chelm who wouldn't go into the water until he learned to swim? Oy, I gave away the punchline. Did I ever tell you why Papa is a baker? When I was small, we were very poor. Not enough to eat, even. If Papa sold umbrellas, there was no rain. If he sold shrouds, suddenly the whole village was healthy and pink. He went to the rabbi—it wasn't a simple problem—and the rabbi said, 'So, be a baker. Like this, at least you'll always have bread in the house.' Wait. It's true . . ."

I ran back into the house. I missed school.

The next day, he wasn't there.

"Schiller's in love."

79

It was Sydney. Miss Prately had asked me a question, and I hadn't heard.

The recital was getting closer and closer. Soon, I'd be up there in front of everybody, and Sydney would be snickering at the back, and Mama and Papa would be ashamed. They'd be sorry they had spent money on school and the lessons and the dress. They would be ashamed I was their daughter.

The day my parcel came, Goldie was with me. We had gone together to the post office to see if there was any mail, a romantic letter for her, or a letter from Mama for me. I hadn't told her about my secret aqua seas. We went to the Krivel's cafe to open the parcel and celebrate at the same time. It was a dress, sent by the Eaton's store in Winnipeg. It was a fairy-tale dress, pink georgette, a gossamer film with the weight of beaded flower patterns on the bodice. We toasted it with a cherry coke.

The next day, there was a letter from Mama.

She and Papa wouldn't be coming to the recital. It would be calving time, and Papa didn't want to leave the birthing to anyone else. They would just have to imagine, she said, how well I would play, and how lovely I would look.

"Cheer up, Schiller," Goldie said. "When everybody sees you in that dress, they'll be as jealous as heck."

"I don't want everybody to be jealous. Except maybe for the snooty mayor's daughter. And even not her, because when people are jealous, they want you to fall flat on your face. I want everybody to be happy for me. If it weren't for you, there wouldn't be anybody."

She looked at me funny, and then she said, "I'm not going."

"You're teasing."

"No, I'm not. I have to take care of the kids."

"But the recital is free. They can go, too."

"The little ones are too squirmy. They always want to go to the bathroom. Anyway, Paul will be there."

"For heaven's sake, I don't know why you keep saying that. I haven't even seen him for weeks."

She was silent.

I left for my lesson.

"Aye," Scotty said, peering at me from under his beetley eyebrows. "You don't look like a lass with much music in her soul. Perhaps I can tempt you with a hot currant scone and a cup of tea instead?"

We sat in the kitchen near the warmth of the cookstove.

"So it is homesickness, then?" he asked.

I got a lump in my throat. I shrugged.

"Aye," he said. "You're too young, too young for that."

"Too young for what?"

"To be hiding yourself from yourself."

"Do you get homesick?" I asked.

"I made a choice, lass," he said, "and now I have a lifetime of pleasure in discovery of what my choice brings. There are a thousand things I would never have known or done if I hadn't followed my fancy out here. And it's time for you to use your imagination. You shouldn't think about the recital at all. You should give it a rest. But you will not. So when you do think about it, dress it up in your mind's eye so you're playing the music of the stars."

As I walked home through the February cold, there was a curtain of water-green and blue-violet northern lights fluttering in the breath of heaven, and I saw myself sitting up in front of the fluttering curtain at a grand piano, and everyone down on earth laughing.

When I walked into the Orpheum Theatre the night of the recital, there wasn't one empty seat. I stood behind the curtain on the stage, took a deep breath, closed my eyes, and tried to see myself playing the music of the stars. Instead, I saw myself tripping as I walked onto the stage, saw myself standing in front of the audience in my torn fairy-tale dress and dumb ox Sydney! laughing at the back of the hall. I ran into the bathroom and threw up.

I waited while the other students played pretty pieces or plunky pieces, but nobody played like the music of the stars. I had wanted Mama and Papa to be proud of me, to see me walking elegantly to the front in my pink beaded movie-star dress and short swingy shiny black hair and black patent shoes and white skin. I had wanted them to hear me playing like the wind in the grasses, like the sun glancing off the blue creek water, like the meadowlarks singing to the sky. I closed my eyes, and I saw the creek, and I felt the wind, and I listened to the notes of my imagination.

"Sara," Scotty said.

I walked to the piano in my movie-star dress. I didn't trip. I sat down to play. I touched the keys. I looked at my fingers. They were white and whole. I struck the first note, and I listened to the notes sing of the wind in the grasses, of the sun glancing off the blue creek water, of a meadowlark singing to the sky . . .

They were clapping like crazy. They liked it. I got up from the piano and walked off the stage and went behind the curtain and cried.

"So?" Goldie asked on the way to school that Monday. "Was it terrible?"

I shrugged.

"Well," Sydney said in a snide tone of voice as I walked into the room, "if it isn't Miss Music Fingers."

But he wasn't snickering.

I walked elegantly to my desk, and melted elegantly into my seat, and ignored everyone—elegantly—all day.

I was on my way back from the post office. My stamps had arrived, sober reds and blues with King George above the palm trees. I was on my way to show them to Scotty. A car slowed behind me. I heard a long, low wolf-whistle, and "Oh, I'm sorry! You have nice legs. We didn't recognize you."

It was one of the Zeisman boys. As he spoke, a head slid below the front seat of the car.

The next day, I waited after school outside Paul's classroom.

"Oh," he said. "It's you."

"And another thing," I said. "Why didn't you want anyone to know you liked me?"

"Nobody goes out with Jewish girls."

"Really? You're the one who's interested in justice for the miners, but Jewish girls aren't good enough for you. You're a bloody little coward. What do you care what people say?"

"Goldie says you're going to marry someone back home."

"She wouldn't say a thing like that."

"Ask her. She says he's going away to study to be a doctor, just like I wanted to."

"But it's not true! Why didn't you ask me?"

"What for? My sister wouldn't lie to me."

I went to Goldie's following the cinnamon to their door, following the noise of the imps to the second floor. "Let me answer!" "No, let me!" I asked for Goldie.

"Why did you lie to Paul?"

"Why should you have a boyfriend? I don't."

"You do so. He writes every week."

"Who told you that?"

"You did."

She laughed.

"I lied," she said. "You're such a hick. You believe anything. I never had a boyfriend in Bromhead. I had to go there because my aunt and uncle said they would pay me for helping them in the store, and Mama and Papa needed the money, so I went. I'm supposed to feel sorry for you because you have to play, and we couldn't afford a piano lesson in a million years, never mind a piano. The first time you played in front of everybody at school—I got you into it, too—I was hoping you'd fall flat on your face. You think you're so smart, always showing off in your Black Bottom sweater up there in the auditorium. I wouldn't have gone to that recital even if you'd paid me. I can hardly wait for you to fail your music-teacher's certificate, and it serves you right I lied to Paul, and I hope you fail all your subjects in school, not just Latin."

She slammed the door. I walked down the steps, out the door, past the cinnamon and raisins, and right into somebody and their loaf of bread.

It was Scotty.

"Tears, is it? And will you be telling me it's 'not bad?'"

"That's what Papa always says."

"Your father is old enough to know what he is saying, and why he is saying it," he said as he wiped my tears. "But when you begin so young, you hide the truth from yourself as well, and that is where the true danger lies."

So I told him about the dreams and the frogs and Sydney and Mrs. Zeisman and Goldie.

"They have empty, tiny souls," he said, "looking for the pain of others to fill their silences. They'll not have a moment's peace in life. You'd best feel sorry for them."

"But what about me? She thinks I'm a rich farm kid, and

I can't even come back to school next year because Mama and Papa can't afford it."

"Have you told your Goldie this?"

I hadn't. And I wouldn't have, either. Not in a million years.

8

Let Me Call You Sweetheart

I was in the post office at the back of Uncle Yacov's store getting ready to sort the mail when I heard someone walking up the wooden sidewalk whistling. "Let Me Call You Sweetheart." In jazz rhythms. The screen door opened, there was a gentle hello to Aunt Sophie, "Let Me Call You Sweetheart" again . . . I buried my head in one of the grey canvas mail bags.

I looked up. It was Meyer, with eyes wide and hurt.

"What are you doing here?"

"Uncle Yacov needed help in the post office."

"Oh."

He watched me sort letters and packages and newspapers into alphabetized boxes.

"Are you glad to be back?"

"Well—"

I gave him his *Estevan Mercury* and a letter from California. He didn't leave.

"I guess," he said finally, "you didn't miss me?"

"Why should I? You aren't speaking to me, remember?"

"But this is a new year. A new rhythm, a new tempo. A new tune."

I laughed. He smiled a wide, honey-warm smile.

The screen door opened again.

"Sara, *medele*!" It was Mr. Shofar in his neatly pressed suit bustling plumply down the aisle toward me. He had arrived the year before to move onto a ready-made farm—barn, granaries, house, pumphouse, ploughed fields, and garden— which the Jewish Colonization Association was renting him. He had been bustling about ever since, and always in a suit. "She grows up before our eyes," he said. "A beautiful woman."

"Thank you, Mr. Shofar."

"Don't thank me. Thank God."

I handed him a fat, important-looking letter from Montreal.

"You see?" He shook it under my nose. "I am not just a farmer. I have important friends. Lawyers write to me."

A little woman with a babushka was looking up at me. Meyer was whistling again, a Yiddish chant for the dead.

"So who are you, tell me?"

"Sara Schiller," I said.

"You're Aaron's girl, or Yacov's?"

"Aaron's."

"So why are you so thin? Your father can't feed you?"

She didn't wait for an answer.

"Who ever heard of Jews on a farm? In the old country we lived in villages like human beings. You looked out the window, there was a house beside, a shop across the street with what to buy. Now, we talk to cows. So? You have something for me? Mrs. Kopelman?"

I gave her the *Yiddish News*.

"That's all? I was expecting maybe a letter from my sister. *Nu*, Sonia. You'll come, you'll visit. I have a boy your age. Who knows? Maybe there'll be something."

I asked Mama about her that evening.

"Oh," she said with a heavy sigh. "The Kopelmans. They're one of the twenty-eight families the Jewish Colonization Association brought in from Poland last spring. They've been the cause of a lot of your father's headaches. Sometimes I think he's too patient and understanding for his own good. So? How was your day at the post office? Did Meyer come in?"

"No," I lied.

She looked disappointed.

At that moment, approaching over the hills, I heard a saxophone playing "A Bicycle Built for Two." In jazz rhythms.

"Sara has a boyfriend, Sara has a boyfriend," the twins sang, running out to meet him.

"Mama!" I said. "Call them back!"

She had disappeared with a basket of ironing. Meyer walked in surrounded by twins. "Meyer's going to marry Sara, Meyer's going to marry Sara . . ."

"You've got a lot of nerve," I said to him.

The brown eyes were wide and hurt again. "Don't you want to marry me?"

"You could have asked me before you told them."

He kissed me. The twins giggled. He blushed, and was gone. The twins went running in to Mama. "Meyer kissed Sara, Meyer kissed Sara. Meyer's going to marry Sara, Meyer's going to marry Sara—"

"She's a lucky girl," I heard Mama say. "He's a lovely boy, and he loves her."

I burst into tears and ran upstairs.

"Sara's crying," the twins announced. "Why is she crying?"

"She's happy," Mama said.

I lay on my bed and tried to decide if I was happy. The kitchen door opened downstairs. It was Ulla. The twins spilled out a jumble of information. "Meyer kissed Sara and he's going to marry her and now she's crying upstairs."

"Oh, Sara!" Ulla bubbled, running up the stairs to sit on the bed and glow at me. "You're so lucky! I can hardly wait to get married! We'll have to sew you a wedding dress, and curtains, and tea towels, and sheets. . . . Sheets!" she said, poking me in the ribs. "What are you crying about?"

"I don't know," I said. "Mama says it's because I'm happy."

"But Meyer does make you happy. You laugh all the time when you're with him."

"I know."

"Well? What more do you want?"

"It's so serious. Getting married is so serious."

"Everything in life is serious. So you might as well enjoy it."

I dreamed about getting married that night. Meyer and I were under the *chupa*, and we had just been married, and it was time to hold hands and walk around the *chupa* seven times.

Everyone was standing around us arguing whether we were supposed to turn to the left or the right.

I told Mama about the dream.

"*Mein Gotte*," she said, and turned pale.

"What's wrong?"

"It's a bad omen. When you dream about a wedding, it's a bad omen."

I laughed.

I didn't see Meyer for two days, not till the next train day when he came in looking shy and embarrassed.

"Everybody says we're getting married," he said.

"Meyer, dummy, that's what happens when you ask someone to marry you."

"They keep asking me when."

"That's a good question," I said. "When?"

"Next week?"

"You can't make a wedding in a week."

"Why not?"

"We have to cook and invite people."

"What's to cook? Your mother will make chicken soup—golden soup to signify riches, and your Aunt Sophie will make 200 cakes—sweet for a sweet life—and my mother will make gefilte fish enough to feed an army. They can do it in two days. And everybody knows already, anyway. Who's to invite?"

"Meyer," I said. "Where are we going to live?"

"With my parents, of course."

"What's wrong with my parents?"

"I don't farm with your parents. I farm with mine."

"When a woman marries a son, she loses a son. When she marries a daughter, she gains a son."

"If you don't want to live with my family, why should I live with yours?"

"People shouldn't get married until they can be responsible for themselves, anyway."

"Don't you want to marry me?"

"Yes. But not if we still have to be children."

"What's going to be?" Mrs. Kopelman had come in. "If you fight like this before, what's going to be after?"

"The same," Meyer said.

"*Mazel tov*," she said. "*Nu*, Sonia—"

"My name is Sara."

"*Nu*, Sonia, you will write for me a letter to the Jewish Colonization Association, they should bring my sister and her family. Why not? The JCA is rich. Why should they be so stingy?"

"Stingy? They bought land for you, built houses for you, gave you horses, cows, ploughs—"

"Ach! They give with one hand and take back with the other."

"What are you talking about? I write all the letters for Papa. I know what you've been given. The only thing the JCA asks is rent to put back into the fund so there'll be more money to help get other Jews out of Europe. Like," I said pointedly, "your sister."

"Listen to her. A little girl with a big mouth."

I gave her a letter from her sister.

She left.

"No wonder Papa has headaches," I said.

"At least she ended our argument," he said. "Bye."

He left whistling "Here Comes the Bride" in jazz rhythms.

When I got home, Mama was writing to her mother and brothers in Los Angeles, worrying about when the wedding would be held, how we would sew enough pillow cases and tea towels in time, and how soon she would be a grandmother.

"Mama," I said. "We don't even have a place to live. How can we get married?"

"You'll live with us. Lots of people start out living with their parents. There's nothing wrong with it."

"You and Papa didn't."

"It was a different time. Your father was homesteading."

"Mama," I said. "We want to start out as adults."

"Don't be silly," Mama said. "You just turned eighteen."

I didn't speak to her for the rest of the evening. Ulla agreed with Mama. A lot of young people did start out with their parents.

There was a package in the mail for Meyer from New York. I called him to tell him.

"Open it," he said. "I don't have any secrets from you."

It was a play in Yiddish from the Maurice Swartz's Yiddish Art Theatre.

"It's about Jewish farmers in the old country," I said. "Let's do it."

"But it's about farmers."

"Yes," I agreed. "Isn't that wonderful?"

"Who's going to want to see a play about farmers?"

"Me," I said. "I'm a farmer."

"I'm not," he said.

"Of course, you are."

"Not forever."

"Who knows what's forever?"

"Marrying you is forever."

"Oh, Meyer," I said. "What a sweet thing to say."

There was a flurry of crackling voices over the telephone. "Quick, come and listen!" "*Mazel tov*." "They're romancing on the telephone. Did you ever hear such a thing?"

"How does your crop look, Mrs. Kopelman?" Meyer asked.

"Don't ask. We work. We slave. Like peasants, we slave. Ten bushels to the acre, and half the JCA steals back."

"You see?" "That's right," other voices joined in.

"Ten bushels to the acre?" Meyer said. "Everybody else thinks we'll get thirty this summer. It's been a good year."

"Good for somebody else is good for somebody else. Since when is that good for us?"

"But we haven't had any hail or grasshoppers. We've had good rain. How could you get only ten?"

"Ten, twenty. What's the difference? We work for the JCA. Not for ourselves. My husband is at the Schillers right now to tell him."

"Aaron Schiller's?" A second voice broke in. "But the doctor is there. He broke his arm."

"No!" A third voice said.

"I heard Mrs. Schiller call the doctor. You weren't listening?"

I hung up.

When I got home, Papa was on the verandah with a cast on his arm. The crank on the tractor had gotten away from him and snapped his arm.

"Was Mr. Kopelman here?" I asked.

90

He nodded.

"What did he want?"

"He came to tell me that he's not going to pay rent to the JCA."

"Why not?"

"As far as he's concerned, the passage from the old country and the land and the house are gifts from Baron de Hirsch, and the JCA has no right to ask for rent."

"What did you say?"

"I said what they already know. Baron de Hirsch set up the Jewish Colonization fund to help Jews live in the New World with self-respect. It was a gift, yes, but a gift that has to be replenished so that it can be given to others."

"What did he say?"

"Nothing."

I gave Papa the play to read.

By the next evening, Mama had also read it, and when Meyer came over, we were ready for him.

"Sara's right," Mama said. "What's wrong with doing something about farmers? It's a romantic story. People like romance."

"This is romantic?" Meyer said. "A young Talmud scholar is visiting from the city, and what happens? He falls in love with the farmer's daughter. If she followed him back to the city, that would be romance. But for him to follow her?"

"What's wrong with that?" I asked.

"It's unnatural. In the Bible, Ruth followed: 'Whither thou goest . . .'"

"Oh," I said. "That's right. She did."

When I got to the post office that Wednesday, Mr. Shofar was already perched on the stool in his neatly pressed suit waiting for his mail. Uncle Yacov had just brought the grey canvas mail bags up from the train.

"Where does the money go?" Mr. Shofar asked as I sorted.

"What money?"

"Miss Innocent. She knows as much as her father. Isn't she the one who writes his letters? The money he collects for the JCA, that's what money."

"It goes to the JCA. Where else would it go?"

"A rich organization like the JCA needs more money?"

"Baron de Hirsch left a sum of money for recolonization. He didn't leave the golden goose."

When I got home, two other Polish settlers were on the verandah arguing with Papa about paying their rent. Papa was explaining all over again how the money had been left to help Jews settle in farming, helping them own land so that they would be able to live and be treated like men, explaining that the money wasn't an endless fund. They said it wasn't true. Papa explained again.

"How do you stand it?" I asked after they had left. "They know all that, and you keep explaining over and over and over. Why are you such a saint? Why don't you just throw them out?"

"I'm not a saint. I understand them, that's all. They've lived all their lives, for generations, like slaves. They've had to survive any way they could with 'You can't travel here,' and 'You can't live there,' and 'You can't go to our schools,' and 'We don't hire Jews.' Why should they believe it when finally they are treated fairly and with respect? It's natural that they don't trust us. They think there's a catch, so they're trying to outsmart us."

The next time I came home, I was just in time to hear Mr. Shofar calling Papa a liar and a thief, and to see Papa stand up and use his good arm to throw him off the verandah.

"Sara," Meyer said. He was waving a book at me. "I have the perfect play. Very romantic. *The Butchery.*"

"Pardon me?" I said. "*The Butchery* is romantic?"

"Yes. Listen." He sat down at the table with me and read while I shaped bread dough into rolls. *The Butchery* was about a sweet young thing who was married off to a nasty old man and murdered him with a butcher knife on their wedding night.

"That's a horrible story. What's wrong with a happy story? A happy, romantic story about people like us?"

"Be reasonable," he said. "A play about Jewish farmers doesn't make sense."

"Why not?"

"Throughout the ages, the highest thing a Jew could do was to become educated."

"Are you saying farmers aren't educated? What do you know about birthing animals and rotating crops?"

"Calm down. I'm talking about book learning."

"You mean book learning for boy Jews. Girls aren't supposed to learn from books, remember? That's one thing I like about this play. It's the girl who wants to take lessons from the scholar. The boys are happy in the fields."

"Exactly. The children in that play are totally uneducated. How can a farmer educate his children in the wilderness? The farmers in that play don't have anyone to teach their children."

"Then why do you say I'm too educated?"

"Jewish education. You can't be a Jew by yourself. It's a social religion. We need a quorum of ten men for prayers."

"Meyer," I said. "Use your head. We're not in the middle of the wilderness. We have a synagogue. We have schools. You know what's wrong with you? You're embarrassed. You're just like the farmers in the play. You think everybody looks down on you because you're a farmer. At school, we always have to learn about England, and rich people, and city people. Why can't we do a play about us?"

"Wait," he said. "We'll see what everybody else wants to do. I bet no one else wants to do a play about farmers, either."

Every train day now, each Monday, Wednesday, and Friday like clockwork, Mr. Shofar bustled plumply into the post office, neatly pressed and suited, and perched on the stool, the picture of the gentleman farmer. He watched as I sorted packages and letters and newspapers; he listened while I translated letters from English to Yiddish; he offered advice as I composed replies.

One afternoon, I set aside a very official letter for Papa. It was from Mr. Shofar's lawyer friend in Montreal. When I turned around, Mr. Shofar had slipped off the stool and was bustling out of the store with a jaunty step. I took the letter home.

Papa read it and passed it on to Mama.

"You're being sued," Mama said with disbelief. "You're being sued for causing Mr. Shofar a concussion. Where did he find a doctor to lie for him?"

Papa shrugged.

"What are we going to do?" Mama asked.

"Go to court, I guess," Papa said. "What else can we do?"

On the next train day, it was Mrs. Kopelman who got there first: "What kind of man would do such a thing?"

"Exactly," I said.

"What? You say such a thing about your own father?"

"No. I say such a thing about Mr. Shofar. He's the one who's spreading lies. Papa's just trying to help the JCA get Jews out of Europe, and Mr. Shofar seems determined to make sure they don't."

Mr. Wilkinson, with his English accent, was right behind her: "You Jews just can't seem to get along."

Mr. Shofar was right behind him: "A thief should be in jail."

"We let you Jews into the country," Mr. Wilkinson announced, "and all you do is cause trouble."

"The only people who belong in this country," I snapped, "are the Indians."

They huffed out of the post office to inform Uncle Yacov that if he didn't get rid of me, their grocery and mail trade would be taken right back to Alkali Flats.

It wasn't long before a second official letter arrived from Montreal. Papa was now being sued for causing Mr. Shofar's daughter a miscarriage. And then there was a third. Papa was being charged as an accomplice of the Jewish Colonization Association in the theft of $124,150 from the new settlers. The first two cases would be tried in Estevan, the third in Montreal. Within two weeks, Mama's short swingy black hair with red lights in it had turned completely white. Papa's headaches were constant. Meyer became agreeable.

"We'll do your play," he said one evening when we were sitting in the kitchen. "We'll do *Green Fields*. After all, it has four concerned, hard-working parents, three good-hearted sincere young men, and two sweet young girls. It'll be a good example, and everyone will remember how nice we can be."

"But a whole bunch of us are rotten," I said. "I'd rather do your play with the nasty old man in it. If the right person plays his part, I'll be the sweet young thing who murders him."

"Sorry," he said. "No one wants to play that part. Even Mr. Shofar won't do it. I asked him."

"Darn," I said.

"If I think any more about the trouble those people are making," Mama said, "I'll go crazy. When are you two getting married?"

I looked at Meyer. He looked at me.

"Rosh Hashonah," Mama said. "By then the trials in Estevan will be over. The new year is a good time for a wedding."

"Mama, we don't have any place to live."

"I told you, you'll live here."

"Meyer doesn't want to live here. He wants me to live with his family."

"Don't be silly," Mama said. "When you marry a daughter, you gain a son. When you marry a son, you lose a son."

"No, Mrs. Schiller," Meyer said. "It would be irresponsible to plan a wedding when we have so much to worry about. And it would be irresponsible of me to marry Sara before I can provide her with a home of her own."

"It isn't good for young people to wait too long before they get married," Mama said.

"Meyer," I said. "Don't you want to marry me?"

"More than anything in the world," he said.

We walked out to the pasture and watched the long evening stretch over the prairie, long colours, rose and gold and scarlet wrapping around the contours of the hills. All of a sudden, he was shy. I teased him, and he kissed me. And we lay together on the sun-warmed grasses.

"*Nu*, Sonia—" It was Mrs. Kopelman. "So you have a surprise."

"I do?"

"Of course. It's normal, a woman gets married, she should have a surprise."

I asked Mama about it that evening.

"Heaven's, no," she said. "We've had too many surprises already this summer."

I took the Dahl's mail over to them. Ulla was knitting.

"Have you heard anything about surprises?" I asked. "Wedding surprises?"

"In Yiddish or English or Swedish?"

"Any of them."

"No. All we talk about here is what cute little dark-eyed musical babies you and Meyer will have."

I blushed.

Meyer hadn't heard of any surprises, either.

"Who'd tell me?" Meyer asked. "If it's a wedding surprise,

I'm supposed to be surprised, too, remember? Ask the twins. They never keep anything a surprise."

"Nobody tells us important things," they said solemnly. "Mama says little girls are dangerous."

Saul was no help, either. He just snorted with disgust. "Girls are crazy. I'd never get married."

The next day, Tsippa was waiting for me in the post office. "You think you're something special, don't you? Just because you're getting married. Any fool can get married. There's no talent in that."

No one came for their mail that day. No one at all. Not Mr. Wilkinson, or Mrs. Kopelman, or Mr. Shofar, or even Meyer. I sat on my stool and imagined Meyer and me married, imagined me cleaning and cooking, changing into a pretty dress just before he came in for supper, like Mama always did for Papa.

"Here Comes the Bride" in schmaltzy waltz broke in.

It was Meyer.

"Come on, baby," he said. "Let's go to the community hall and make music."

"There's no piano. And I'm hungry."

"We are in love," he said sternly. "We don't need food."

But there was a piano in the community hall. It was our piano from our living room.

"What's going on?" I asked.

"You 'n me, baby. We's music, baby—" He sat me down at the piano and as he raised the saxophone to his lips to begin a rousing march, the door burst open, and the whole community came marching in, single file—Mr. and Mrs. Shofar, Mr. and Mrs. Wilkinson, Mr. and Mrs. Kopelman and little round Moishe, Uncle Yacov and Aunt Sophie and Tsippa, Mr. and Mrs. Dahl . . . marching single file to the front of the hall and placing on the stage a cup and saucer or an embroidered tea towel or a pair of salt and pepper shakers, a cake, a package of sandwiches—until it was filled with food and gifts, and Meyer and I played while the whole community danced at our shower. It was about time, Mama said, that we had something to be happy about.

"*Nu*, Sonia," Mrs. Kopelman said. "Did you ever hear such a business? Everybody's going to Estevan to the trial. Even my

Moishela. I ask him, 'How can we afford?' and he tells me Hymie Shofar invites everybody. His friend, the lawyer from Montreal, invites, and he pays. *Nu*? So when is the wedding?"

"After the trial."

"After the trial? Your father will be in jail after the trial. What kind of wedding is it without the father?"

"Oh, don't worry," I said sweetly. "My father will be here. But I hope you won't be too disappointed."

"How can we be disappointed? Hymie Shofar is in this country for years before us. If he says your father is in jail, he will be in jail."

"Years? He told you he's been here for years? He came in 1927, one year before you. Since when is one year 'years'?"

All of the new Jewish settlers, all those who believed Mr. Shofar had been there for years, were going to Estevan for the trial. They going as moral support for the Shofars, and they were staying at the Empress Hotel as guests of the Montreal lawyer's mother. Papa wouldn't let anyone go for him except Uncle Yacov and me. Mama wasn't feeling well, and Papa didn't want any of the farmers wasting their time.

The morning of the trial, a hot August morning, we had a good breakfast at our hotel, The International, to keep up our strength, Papa said. Uncle Yacov was afraid that a sense of humour was going to be more important than strength.

The Miscarriage, the Disappearing Baby, was first. It seemed like all of Estevan was there except for Scotty and my ramrod-straight principal. Prim and plump Miss Prately, the dentist and the dentist's wife, the doctor's daughter and Miss Wrong Note and Goldie . . . Uncle Yacov said they must have closed down the town for the event. Paul was there to translate. I introduced him to Meyer. Meyer told him we were getting married. Paul asked him if he was going to be a doctor. Meyer laughed.

The daughter-in-law, quiet and meek and with her eyes too close together, was called to speak first.

"He's a murderer," she told the Montreal lawyer, a sympathetic young man in a dapper navy suit. "I told him we couldn't pay the rent for the farm, and he pushed me."

"How did he push you?"

"In the stomach. What do you think happened? A mis-

carriage. In the middle of the yard with cows and horses looking."

Our lawyer, who looked worried instead of dapper, got up.
"How tall are you?"

"What's that got to do?" she asked.

"Would you stand, please?"

She stood.

"About four-foot-ten. My client is about five-foot-six. It
would be very awkward for a man so much taller to push a
woman in the stomach, wouldn't it?"

"That's what I said myself," she said. "I said, 'The man is
crazy. He'll do anything.' He tried to kill my father-in-law. Why
shouldn't he kill me?"

Her doctor was called, a doctor from Estevan, fifty miles
from Short Haul. Her doctor was not Doctor Lowe, only twelve
miles away from Short Haul. Not Doctor Lowe, who, paid a
monthly retainer by the JCA, treated the entire community, Jew
and non-Jew alike, for free.

"Yes," the doctor said. "I examined her two weeks ago."

"Was she pregnant?"

"No."

"Has she miscarried?"

"I couldn't tell. It was too long after the event."

"But she could have miscarried, and you wouldn't have
been able to tell?"

"Yes."

There were audible sighs and wriggles and expressions of
pleasure in the courtroom.

"Is this the first time," our worried Estevan lawyer asked
when things had settled down, "that you have examined this
woman?"

"No, I examined her once last year."

"What did you examine her for?"

"She was concerned because she had been married for
three years and still wasn't pregnant."

"And what did you tell her?"

"I told her that as far as I could tell, she would never be able
to have a child."

I laughed.

The Shofar supporters glared at me. I laughed all through

98

lunch. Uncle Yacov told me not to count my chickens before they were hatched. No matter what happened, he said the Jewish community did not need this kind of publicity: the Canadian government was always looking for excuses and ways to keep Canada pure, pure white and Christian. Papa had a migraine headache.

That afternoon, Mr. Shofar bustled with plump importance to the stand and told us that Mr. Schiller had thrown him off the verandah for no reason. Now, he, Mr. Shofar was useless on the farm. He had to leave everything to his son: he couldn't help with the haying, he had headaches, his memory wasn't so good . . .

"Normally," our Estevan lawyer said, "Mr. Schiller is a very calm man. What did you do to make him so angry?"

"He's crazy, that's all."

"Who put in your crop last year?"

"My son."

"Did you have a concussion last year?"

"I had business in Montreal."

"Who took off your crop last year?"

"My son."

"I see," our Estevan lawyer said. "So it is usual that you cannot do your own farming."

Mr. Shofar's doctor was called. It was not Dr. Lowe, nor was it the Estevan doctor. It was the Weyburn doctor, also fifty miles away from Short Haul.

"Yes," the doctor said, "there is something wrong with Mr. Shofar's head."

"So Mr. Shofar's statement that he suffered a concussion when Mr. Schiller pushed him is correct?"

"There is something wrong with his head," the doctor repeated, "but it has nothing to do with a fall."

"There," I said to Meyer, "now we can get married."

"It's about time," he said, "that we had a little enthusiasm."

None of the Polish settlers congratulated Papa, and they still didn't want to pay their rent to the JCA.

The post office had been quiet all week.

"Who would believe?" Mrs. Kopelman said. "Who would believe a doctor would lie like that?"

99

I handed her a letter. It was in English from Ottawa.
"Read for me."

I read it. Her application to have her sister and her family
accepted into Canada had been refused.

She left in tears.

Papa had a letter from Ottawa, too, also from the Department of Immigration. There had been complaints from our
community about the new settlers: why should Canada accept
more Jews when all they did was cause trouble?

That evening, I was sitting on the verandah crocheting a
doily for the top of the piano that I might someday have. Papa
had been in Montreal for the trial for over a week, and the
harvest was over, and there was nothing to do but worry.

I heard "Bicycle Built for Two," in schmaltzy waltz.

"Here comes Sara's husband, here comes Sara's husband,"
the twins chorussed.

"Sonia, *medele*, your mother is right. Young people
shouldn't wait too long to get married. We will get married as
soon as your father is back."

"We will?"

"Yes."

"Why?"

"Because you are young and desirable, and I am young and
I desire you."

"We still don't have any place to live."

"We aren't going to live here. We're going to live in Los
Angeles."

"We are?"

"Yes. We are."

"Why?"

"Because I like selling insurance better than I like farming."

"How could you like selling insurance better than farming?"

"Easy. I sit behind a plough and the grain just curls up and
goes to sleep. Horses sit down and laugh. Meadowlarks use my
head for a telephone pole."

"You're ashamed of being a farmer, like the Kopelmans. We
should have done that play. You needed it more than anyone
else. Maybe you would have seen what the scholar saw when
he decided to stay in the country, what the farmers finally saw

100

for themselves. They are fine people, those farmers, and they are Jews, like any other Jews. You can be a Jew in the city and starve, you know. At least on the farm there's always food on the table."

"Yes, and blizzards, and not enough rain, and too much rain. Sara, I don't want to depend on the sky for my living."

"What about Papa?"

"Nothing's going to happen to Papa. Those people are idiots. Shofar will probably get himself deported."

"Why? How do you know?"

"Your father and the JCA kept records of everything, didn't they? The elevator agents have records of everything, too. Even when Mr. Kopelman says he only got ten bushels to the acre, there are records at the elevator that they delivered thirty bushels."

"But I don't want to move."

"I'm going as soon as we've done the play. I have a job offer, and if I stay until spring, I'll be caught by ploughing and seeding and calving, and I'll never get out."

"Out?"

"Out. Away from here. What's the matter with you? You've been complaining all summer about 'these people.' Why would you want to stay?"

"I want to help."

"You have your own life to live."

"This is my life."

"It is? Explain it to me. I'm not a stupid man. Explain it. You said you couldn't stand to see what 'these people' were doing to your parents, and now you're letting them ruin our lives."

"Moses made the slaves from Egypt wander the deserts for forty years until the people who had lived and thought like slaves died off. He took the children of freedom into the promised land. Wait. You'll see what their children will become."

"I'm not waiting."

"If I were a man, I would love to be a farmer."

"You're not a man."

"I could be a farmer's wife, though."

"Then you can't be my wife, because I'm not going to be a farmer."

He left. We did the play about the farmers—about us—without him. Tsippa was the farmer's daughter who married the scholar. She said I had the shortest engagement in history.

9

Schoolteachers

"Gee," Angela said. "We've been here for twenty-four hours. Do you think we're going to like it?"

"Like what?"

I'd been staring at the brick wall—the view through the tiny window above our kitchen sink. Angela Lowe was lying on her back on the couch in the living room, her too-long legs dangling over the end. With her blond hair fluffed around her head, and her blue eyes innocent, she looked just like her name. It was disgusting.

"Jeepers, isn't it exciting? Do you think we're going to like everything?"

"What everything?"

"Oh—living by ourselves, and being in a big city like Regina, and going to Normal School . . ."

"And not seeing our family for three months, and studying and cooking and cleaning—I'll like it if we get a school to teach in somewhere next year."

"You will. You'll teach at Cactus Hill."

"How do you know?"

"Because your Dad's the chairman of the Cactus Hill Schoolboard, and I heard him tell Daddy he didn't want to have

103

any more complaints from the school inspector about inadequate teaching in his school."

"But what if I'm inadequate, too? What if we don't even pass Normal?"

"Then we'll get a job at the Five and Dime instead," she said dreamily. "I'll sell hats, and I'll wear a different one every day."

"Angela, there's a depression. Nobody has any work."

"But wouldn't you love to live here? Just think, sixty thousand people. I bet we could get to know a different new person here every day for a hundred years. And I bet there are thousands of good-looking men, too. At home, Mama wouldn't let me put my nose past the door after eight o'clock. Can't you hardly wait till tomorrow?"

"I can hardly wait so much I feel sick," I said. "College isn't like high school."

"I know," she sighed happily. "We're adults."

The next morning, we were walking down College Avenue and up a tree-lined walk, part of an ever-growing flock of hundreds of students funneling into the central tower of a long, two-storey red brick building. We found ourselves in an assembly hall with majestic high ceilings. "It's like a castle," I said. "Golly," Angela said. "Look at all those men." A chord was struck on the piano. We rose to sing "God of Our Fathers." It wasn't my faith, but it was someone's: I sang, too.

"Our children are our future." (We were being welcomed to Regina Normal School.) "You have their morality, their personalities, their future, in your hands. In a province as young as ours, in a time of depression and drought, you may never be needed as much as you are today. You have indeed chosen a proud profession. Next year, the 300 young men and women I see before me—302 to be exact—will be welcoming their own students into three hundred and two schools throughout Saskatchewan."

By lunchtime we had been introduced to all our subjects— art, music, science, health science, psychology, penmanship, history of education, social sciences, and languages—and had been assigned to our classrooms in rooms A to G. Angela and I were together in Room B. She stayed to sign up her long legs for basketball. I didn't sign up for orchestra. For once, I could listen and watch like everyone else. I didn't have to play and no one could make me. I was an adult.

The next day we sat, forty-five of us, in Room B, silent, expectant. Angela poked me and pointed. He was blond, sun-streaked blond, with eyes that were a startling blue in a sun-browned face. She pointed again, and giggled. One of the women was wearing a pair of farmer's blue denim overalls.

A pretty little dark-haired woman wafted into the room. "Stand, class," she said, smiling gently at each of the men in turn. The men smiled back. "Breathe. Stretch and breathe. Stretch, and breathe deeply. Sing," she said, opening a pretty little mouth and uttering a trill. "Like that." We sang like that. "Now, one at a time . . ."

By the end of the class, we had been categorized—bass, tenor, alto, soprano—strong singers at the back, weak singers at the front, and she was smiling gently once again at the men. "There is nothing I have done with you today that you cannot do in your own classrooms."

She was gone. A wide, bald head poked around the door. "Here's me head, me feet's comin'." The body followed, a slouching illustration, into the room. "Don't go through life like that. Walk with pride. Show the world that you know what you're about." He approached, stood erect in front of the class. "Students," he said with a zealous gleam in his eye, "we have a job to do. We will eradicate 'ain't' and 'seen' from the face of Saskatchewan. 'He ain't goin',' 'I seen him' will be a thing of the past. Drill," he said. "That's the ticket. 'I *am not* going,' 'He *isn't* going,' 'You *are not* going,' 'I *saw* him,' 'You *saw* him,' 'She *saw* him' . . . If you say the right thing often enough, it becomes right."

"But, sir—" It was Him of the startling blue eyes.

"Yes, Mr. Hesla?"

"It will never work, sir."

"Am I teaching this class, or are you?"

"You are, sir. It will work with us because we believe you. But the children won't believe us."

"I suppose you—an untrained teacher—have had experience with the children in the schools?"

"Yes, sir. There weren't any trained teachers available, so I was given a temporary certificate. I tried teaching 'ain't' ain't a word. The kids thought it was funnier than a hog walking on two legs. And then one of the seven-year-olds crossed her arms and said, 'My mother says "ain't." That was the end, sir. They never believed another word I said."

After classes, Angela stayed for the first basketball practice. I walked downtown past large houses with elegant verandahs to buy our psychology and history of education books.

"Saskatchewan is starving," Angela announced as we sat down to supper. "If we don't do something soon, we'll all go down with the ship."

"Since when are you interested in politics?"

"This isn't politics. This is our lives. There's a Farmer–Labour meeting tonight. You should come with me. You're a farmer."

"You're not."

"I know. But Saskatchewan is an agricultural economy. We all depend on the farmer."

"What about our penmanship assignment? We're supposed to re-copy the whole book for tomorrow."

"'Good teachers have well-rounded o's and evenly slanted t's and j's,'" she said, mimicking Head-First-Feet's-Comin's zeal. "What an assignment."

She was on her way out the door.

"Hey, I cooked. The least you can do is hang around long enough to do the dishes."

"I'll do them when I come back."

I was asleep by the time she got home. When I got up, she was asleep. I washed the dishes so I could have breakfast.

The bald head poked around the door. "Here's me head . . ." By the time his feet had followed, Mr. Hesla had a question for him. "Sergeant Major Bellamy, what do you think of the Farmer–Labour Party? What do you think of their land-lease program?"

"It will never work."

"I've been to a few of their meetings, sir, and as I understand it, if a farmer were about to lose his farm to a mortgage company, the government would take over the mortgage to pay it off and hold the land for the farmer. The farmer would lease the land for as long as he or his descendants wanted to use it. The mortgage companies would have their mortgages paid off, the farmer wouldn't lose his farm, and the province wouldn't lose the land. Everybody would be happy."

"If everyone would be so all-fired happy, why isn't the Farmer–Labour Party winning elections?"

"Because the opposition calls it communism, and as soon as people hear the word, they run scared. Personally, I don't care what the labels are, as long as it works. We're on a sinking ship, and we might as well try to swim."

"You Farmer–Labour people. Thick-headed dreamers," Head-First snorted. "You think you can have crop insurance, accident insurance, old-age insurance, unemployment insurance . . . Hell will freeze over before that happens. Discussion closed."

"Sinking ships?" I teased Angela on the way home.

"So what?"

"That wouldn't be the reason you're so interested in the Farmer–Labour party all of a sudden, would it?"

"So what if it is? Everybody learns something from somebody. And it wouldn't hurt if you had a boyfriend, either."

"How do you know?"

"You wouldn't be in such a bad mood all the time."

I took a deep breath. Dr. Lowe had made me promise to take care of her; I was two years older than she was . . .

"I'm going to the Five and Dime to see if I can find anything for our music project. Do you want to come?"

"Which music project?"

"We only have one. To make a rhythm section for primary students out of stuff we have around the house. Remember? She gave it to us this morning."

"If I go with you, you should go with me to the meeting tonight."

"I can't. I have to wash some clothes. I'm all out."

"You never think about anybody but yourself."

"Who washed the floors and cleaned the bathroom? And who does all the cooking? I could cook just for myself, you know. I don't have to cook for you."

"Who asked you?" she snapped. She ran on ahead.

I wandered along kicking dry leaves, and I came back from the Five and Dime without any bright ideas at all. I sat at the table and looked out the kitchen window at our brick wall. Angela's dirty dishes were on the table, her toast-crumb saucer perched on the jam can. It looked like a drum, that bronze can, a drum with a white saucer top. I picked up the knife and fork Angela had left on the table and tapped on my drum. I could stretch some white cotton across the top, sugar-sack cotton, maybe, and varnish it . . .

I thanked Angela for not doing her dishes.

One week later, I found a note from her on the table: "Mother is coming."

"Angela," I said, "isn't your mother going to think it's kind of funny that we're not talking to each other?"

"She knows."

"Is that why she's coming?"

"It would be nice to have someone to talk to."

"You stopped talking to me. I didn't start it."

"You complain all the time. What am I supposed to do?"

"Oh, brother," I said.

A week later, Mrs. Lowe was standing at the door. Angela got up off the couch and flung herself into her mother's arms and burst into tears. Mrs. Lowe glared at me over her daughter's shoulder. She was just in time for supper.

"Just imagine," Mrs. Lowe said as I served the chicken stew, "Tsippa getting married before you girls."

"Tsippa's getting married?" I said. "Who's she marrying?"

"A young man here at the teacher's college. Barney something."

"He's the one who borrowed Sara's penmanship assignment to hand in because he was too lazy to do it himself," Angela said. "He never said anything to us."

"Men don't talk about these things like women do, dear," Mrs. Lowe said. "Sara's poor mother is just worried to death. I told her she's being foolish. Sara's only twenty-one, after all. There's still a chance."

She went off to the bedroom—Angela's bed in Angela's and my bedroom, the only bedroom—to read. Angela would sleep on the couch, though really, Mrs. Lowe said, with her long legs, the couch would suit me better.

It was midnight by the time I got to bed. Mrs. Lowe was in Angela's bed propped up by both our pillows surrounded by two million magazines. At one in the morning, she told me that Jeanette Luff had started out playing the piano in a Saskatchewan movie house, and now she was Cecil B. DeMille's darling, and she wasn't even as pretty as Angela or I. At two a.m. she read me recipes for chocolate snickerdoodles and salmon aspic. At 3 a.m. she gave me home remedies for bedwetting and sore throats.

The next day, Head-First-Feet's-Comin' stopped me in the hall. "By jiminy, Miss Schiller," he said. "You're just the person I wanted to see. Miss Lowe tells me you play a pretty good piano. I have a piece I haven't heard since my wife passed away. Miss Lowe says it would be no trouble for you at all."

"As long as it's not anything by Chopin."

"No, no. Nothing like that. 'Finlandia' by Sibelius."

I had never heard of "Finlandia." I didn't have a piano, and I certainly didn't have the music. The school had a piano, though. And Sergeant Major Bellamy had the music.

"Finlandia" turned my stomach. It was complicated and beautiful. It reminded me of snarled crochet thread. It reminded Sergeant Major Bellamy of pine forests and leaping salmon and mushroom salads.

"Angela," I said when I got home. "That wasn't very nice of you."

"What?" she asked innocently.

"To tell Sergeant Major Bellamy that I loved giving public performances. Why do you think I didn't join the college orchestra?"

"I couldn't help it. Whenever he talks about his dear departed wife, he looks so cute."

"How would you like to get up in front of 302 students plus all our teachers?"

"I do. I play basketball."

"Now, Sara dear," Mrs. Lowe called from the bedroom. "She was just trying to help."

I fried eggs for supper and sat at the table reading about Cheetah the monkey in my psychology of education book.

We had to observe in the schools for a week, and after five nights of Mrs. Lowe's reading, I was exhausted. I climbed the steps to my assigned school, a brown brick two-storey building, and entered a wide cool hallway. I knocked on the door with a six on it. A tall bony woman—the witch who ate Hansel and Gretel a thousand years ago—stood in the doorway.

"Miss Webster?"

"Aye?"

"I'm your student teacher." She looked hungry. "Sara Schiller."

"If you arre planning to teach childrren," she announced—I could hear the oven door in the background—"you had betterr get rrid of that accent."

I turned on my heel and walked down the hallway. The door—the oven door with innocent grade sixes being turned to gingerbread—slammed behind me. I marched straight back to the college and up to the principal's office.

"Excuse me," I said. "Do I have an accent?"

"Oh, dear," he said mildly. "You have been assigned to Miss Webster's room. Of course you don't. She does. But she thinks she brought Scotland with her. Take the day off. We'll reassign you."

I went home to sleep. Mrs. Lowe was still in bed, but she woke up long enough to announce that we were almost out of supplies.

"But we can't be. My parents sent enough food for another two weeks."

"Well, dear. Food goes."

"But—"

She had gone back to sleep.

Mama and Papa were going to be upset. Dr. Lowe was paying for the apartment, and we were supplying the food. But the farm had to supply our family and Uncle Yacov's family as well.

I was reassigned to the same brick school to a grade four class with a pretty, young, and unaccented teacher.

"Miss Schiller," one of the students piped up brightly, "is there a cure for cancer?"

"No," I said gently. "I'm afraid there isn't."

"Miss Schiller," the unaccented teacher protested excitedly, "you are misleading the children. At this very moment, my brother is at work in Ontario looking for a cure for cancer. What you should have said was, 'Not yet, but, hopefully, there will be soon.'"

I looked at my innocent grade fours with new eyes. They had set me up.

Within a week, there was more food from home, and a letter from Mama asking what was going on. I wrote back: Mrs. Lowe cooked more than we needed at one time, cooked it till it was mush, served more than we ate, and threw out what we didn't. Dr. Lowe wrote asking her to come home. She took her *Ladies Home Journals* and her *True Confessions* and her *Mayfairs* and *Liberty* magazines with her. A few days later, Dr. Lowe was at our door.

"Daddy!" Angela said, and leaped into his arms.

"I've come to cheer my babies up," he said, "and we'll start by going out to dinner. But first—"

He pulled out presents. Drumsticks and wooden clappers Saul had made for me, and a drum for Angela, wooden with real parchment stretched across the top, painted red and trimmed with gilt. The Alkali Flats Citizens' Band had made it for her.

"Don't you feel guilty, Daddy?" Angela asked cheerfully as we settled down into soft chairs at a table set with white linen and silverware. "Bringing us to the Saskatchewan Hotel when people have to catch gophers for dinner?"

"I've done my share. I worked my way through medical school teaching in one-room schools, and these days I get paid in chickens and eggs."

"But the cost of this meal could feed a whole family for a week."

"I see," he said sternly. "It's those meetings. I thought you had given them up to concentrate on college instead."

"Oh, Daddy! Nobody ever fails Normal. Besides, people are starving, and mortgage companies are forcing farmers off their farms. It's not bad weather, Daddy. It's the banking system and their mortgage companies. We have to do something."

"Look here, young lady. I sent you to Normal School to become a teacher, not to spend your time at meetings. Your mother is at home worrying herself sick because you're not married yet, while you're going to meetings."

"Jeepers, I'm not worried," Angela said. "There are handsome men wherever you look."

"Handsome is as handsome does. And that goes for you, too."

It wasn't until dessert that he brought it up.

"So what's going on?"

"What do you mean?" we chorussed guiltily.

"You're not getting along," Dr. Lowe said. "Sara writes home that you never help in the apartment, Angela, and you write that Sara picks on you."

"She does," Angela said.

"I do not," I said. "I just want you to do something around the apartment."

"But you want the dishes done right away," Angela said. "I do them. I don't have to do them when you want."

"Look," Dr. Lowe interrupted. "We're not here. We don't know what goes on. You girls have your whole lives ahead of you. In a few months, you'll go your separate ways. All of this will mean nothing to you. But it could break up the friendship Aaron and I have, and if you break us up at this time of life, we'll have no one. I'm pleading with you. Don't do this to us."

"Gee, Daddy," Angela said.

He handed us both a handkerchief.

The next evening Angela was helping me peel potatoes.

"I don't know how you do it so fast. You're already finished yours, and I'm only half-finished mine."

"Oh, well," I shrugged. "Speed isn't what counts in most things. It's doing a good job."

"Gee, Sara. You've never said anything like that to me before." She pondered. "I'm sorry I got you into playing for the assembly."

"Me, too," I said. "Maybe I'll die before then."

"Don't say things like that! It could happen."

"I was only joking. I wouldn't mind a broken arm, though."

"Hey, Schiller!"

It was Barney, my future cousin-in-law. He handed me my penmanship notebook with a look of disgust. "When I asked if I could borrow it to hand in, you said you got a B-plus on it, and that guy from Room A got an A for it. I got a D."

I stifled a giggle.

"You won't laugh when you don't have a job next year. After Tsippa and I are married, I'm getting the job at Cactus Hill."

"Don't be too sure. They want a good teacher, and your record doesn't sound so good."

"If I don't, Tsippa doesn't get married."

"I don't think she's that desperate."

"Think again," he said. "We'll see who laughs last."

When Angela came home from her basketball game, I was still mad.

"You should tell Tsippa," Angela said. "What if she does marry him? He doesn't even like her."

"She won't believe me. She hated me before she even learned to walk. And I don't like her much, either."

"Then tell her parents. After all, if he's marrying her just to get a job—"

"They'll think I want the job. And if he doesn't marry her, Aunt Sophie and Tsippa will blame it on me."

Head-First-Feet's-Comin' was all excited. Psychologists had just figured out how we should mark our exams.

"We know we are not all sergeant-major material. We just have to look around us. Some of us just have to look at ourselves."

"Darn tootin'," Mr. Hesla muttered.

"Psychologists have figured out that when you test populations of 100, you get a curve on the graph shaped like a bell, with a few people on one side of the bell, the left bottom edge, of below-average intelligence, and about the same number on the other side with above-average intelligence. However, most people are part of the bulging bubble in the middle, like you ladies and gentlemen. Imagine if you laid me across the table. My feet would be below average, my bulging belly in the middle, which is most of my profile, would be you, and my head would be above average. Take it from me. If your students write an exam, and they all get 90 percent, there is something wrong with your exam."

"But, sir," Hesla said. "None of us will ever have 100 students in a class. I've never had more than 30. How do I know, sir, that I don't have the top end of the 100? Or all the middle so that everybody gets 65 percent? Or all at the bottom end, for that matter? The psychologists are probably talking about averages, sir. When I take a crop off, I get an average of fifteen bushels to the acre, and on a good year, twenty-five. But that doesn't mean every field has the same yield. The south quarter always has a higher yield than the north quarter."

"You finished, Mr. Hesla?"

"Yes, sir. That's all I'm saying, sir. It might not be the test at all. It might be that all my students are bright. It might even be that I found a way to make it so interesting that all my students understood it. And remembered."

"Let me tell you," Head-First-Feet's-Comin' drew himself up to his full five-foot-three-inch height, "we've done intelligence tests on all of you, and you sure fit the model."

"But there are 300 of us in the college, sir. And I'm willing to bet my bottom dollar, not every class has the same make-up."

"Well, you sure as heck are the most annoying young man in the college, by a long shot."

"There you are, sir."

"Guess what!" Angela said coming in after one of her basketball practices. "Barney's telling everyone he's got the job at Cactus Hill School. What if we both don't get jobs? Lars is right. The government should make sure there are jobs for people. Or they should have support for us when there aren't. What do women do if there's no work? Can't you just see me and you riding the rails?"

And she burst into tears.

"Angela, don't be silly. We'll stay home, that's all. Our parents can afford to keep us."

"Forever?" she sniffled. "Mr. Douglas, that preacher from Weyburn, came to the last meeting, and he went to Chicago last summer, and there were thousands and thousands of people living in lean-tos along the railroad tracks. The men go into the city to beg or steal during the day, and at night the police herd them back out. The only difference between Mr. Douglas and those men was that he had a job, and they didn't. There were lawyers, and bank clerks, and dentists, and railroad workers, and doctors . . . He said that out here it's natural to blame the weather, but in a place like that, it's easy to see it's a man-made catastrophe."

114

"There's nothing we can do about it."

"People are starving, and farmers are losing their farms."

"Angela, I know all that."

"You don't care. All you do is study."

"Don't you think teaching is helping?"

"But what if there's no work? You don't even have a job now."

"Angela, stop it! I'm scared enough already."

"Lars says being scared doesn't help. He says we're all going to have to help with the election next year. And we need a teachers' federation. Teachers have no protection. Lars got called to the home of the chairman of his school: he had to walk three miles there and back after teaching all day just because the chairman had heard that he had been seen with a woman wearing lipstick. And do you know what a lot of schoolboards are doing? They advertise a job at $200 a year, and when you get there, they say it was a mistake: $100 plus room and board, take it or leave it. And the $200 is the yearly grant from the provincial government."

"What do you know about science experiments we can do in our classrooms with material we have around the yard?"

"Why?"

"Because we're supposed to have ideas for science class tomorrow."

"See? It's just like I said. All you ever do is worry about yourself. Nobody ever fails Normal School, anyway."

I had a dream that night that I was eradicating "ain't" from Cactus Hill School, and none of the students would listen, and all of the parents hated me, and Papa fired me and gave the job back to Barney, and Angela and I were riding the rails in a blizzard, and Angela was crying.

I woke up.

Angela was crying.

"Angela, what's wrong?"

"Mind your own business."

"Are you afraid you won't get a job?"

"No."

"Are you homesick?"

"No."

"Are you mad at me?"

115

"No."

"Then what's wrong?"

"Lars. He's married. That woman who was wearing lipstick is his wife. She's a teacher, too. I knew it was too good to be true—good-looking, and smart, and liking me."

"But he is good-looking, and he is smart, and he does like you."

"How do you know?"

"Besides, it's not his fault he's married."

"He could have told me. He should have told everybody."

"They have to keep his marriage secret, or she'll lose her job. Married women aren't allowed to teach, remember?"

"I hate him, anyway. He should have told me."

"He did."

"But now it's too late. I love him."

She cried most of the night.

The next morning, our music teacher wafted into the room and smiled gently at all the men.

"Why don't we have an exam this morning? Just a little one, to see if we've learned the techniques of teaching music and singing to our little ones."

There was a *thunk* behind me, and Angela was running out of the room. I turned around to see one of the students on the floor. It was Miss Eilertson, the girl who had been wearing her father's overalls all year. Angela came running back in with her cardigan dripping with water and placed it on her forehead. Eilertson opened her eyes and asked if she were dead, and when Angela said she wasn't, she started to cry. Lars picked her up and carried her out. Angela followed.

"Dear me," our pretty little music teacher worried. "We can't have our exam after all this, can we? I don't suppose we feel much like singing . . ."

Angela was back at the door. She beckoned. She looked shaken.

"What's wrong? She's not dead, is she?"

"The principal just gave us five dollars."

"What for?"

"To relax. He says Miss Eilertson is terrified of exams, and we're supposed to take her for lunch and a matinee."

"Yippee!"

As soon as we set foot out of the castle door into the mild and lovely December morning, tears welled up in Miss Eilertson's eyes.

"See?" she said. "It's a beautiful day. That means we won't get any rain this year. It should be cold and thirty below and snowing."

"It's not the weather," Angela comforted her. "One of the farmers at the Farmer–Labour meetings north of here—they've had rain but there's nowhere to sell their crops. He shipped fourteen head of cattle to Winnipeg and got only three or four cents a pound. It just barely covered the shipping costs."

"Angela!" I said.

"So even if it rains," Miss Eilertson sobbed, "we'll still lose the farm."

We went for lunch. Almost everything we tried to talk about—men, weather, or college—made one or the other of us cry. We ate corned beef on rye and pie and ice-cream in silence.

"Gee," Lilly Eilertson sighed, "I haven't eaten this much in—I never want to be hungry again."

"Don't they feed you where you board?" Angela asked.

"Sort of," she said. "I don't eat with them. Isn't it time for the movie?"

"Imagine being as beautiful as Greta Garbo," Angela sighed on the way out of the theatre. "If I ever met anyone as handsome as Lionel Barrymore, I'd die."

Lilly was sniffling again. It was snowing big, soft, fluffy snowflakes out of violet skies. I slipped and fell on a wax-paper bread wrapper. I sat there, stunned.

"Oh, my God," Angela said. "Are you all right?"

I wriggled my wrist. The pain brought tears to my eyes. I laughed.

"Are you in shock?" Angela asked.

"Isn't it wonderful? I won't be able to play 'Finlandia.'"

Lilly was sniffling again.

"What's wrong?" Angela and I chorussed as she helped me up.

"The people I board with. It's five o'clock, and I should have been home right after classes."

"It's none of their business."

117

"Yes, it is. I'm working for my room and board, and they're having people over tonight." Now she was really crying. "They have people over every night, and I can't go to bed until the kitchen is clean, and I can never clean it because nobody leaves until at least midnight. I'm so tired I could die."

"You can stay with us," I said, "can't she, Angela?"

"Really?" Lilly asked, and she cried even harder.

We walked home through a snowflake world. By the end of the week, we were all sharing clothes, Lilly and I were cooking, and Angela learned how to do dishes and wash a floor.

Our pretty little teacher had wafted into the room. She stood, smiling bravely, sorrowfully, at each of the men in turn.

"I know you will understand," she said softly, "when I tell you that I have been deeply offended." She drew a deep and troubled breath. "We have just had a meeting to award the prize for the musical instruments you submitted. Sergeant Major Bellamy voted for you, Miss Lowe, but—gee, I just don't know where the average teacher would find real parchment and gilt paint. We expected great things from you, Mr. Hesla, but, of course, you failed to do the assignment at all. We all have problems. We understand that. But your students won't. We had no choice but to award the prize to Miss Schiller. Your jam-can drum and pie-plate cymbals showed imagination, but I am offended that you did not put more work into it. You did not give my assignment the respect it deserved."

"Excuse me," Angela said sweetly. "We were told that children are happy with simple toys and instruments. What exactly would you have liked Miss Schiller to have done with a pie plate and jam can?"

Barney stopped me in the hall on the way out. He had heard the good news. "Too bad," he said, "you won't have a school next year to put all that imagination into."

We were celebrating the end of term in our tiny kitchen with the brick-wall view. Snowflakes smashed themselves against the brick.

We had had the final assembly, and Angela had come through it like one of the people on the bottom edge of the bell curve—above average. Mr. Hesla had spoken on the need

118

for a teachers' federation, and she listened as if he were no one special at all. She was the first of the 301 of us to sign. Lilly wrote her exams without above-average terror. Our pretty little teacher had wafted onto the stage and played "Finlandia." It still reminded me of snarled crochet thread. We would be leaving the next day, 302 student teachers praying for 302 schools at a time when our province never needed us more.

We made a toast to floating ships.

10

Flowers in the Sky

"Sara, you're back!" Tsippa said.

She was sitting behind her mother's cash register. With the evening summer sun streaming in on her red-gold hair and accenting her grey eyes, she was radiant and lovely.

I agreed that I was back.

"Isn't it wonderful?" she said excitedly. "We're going to get married in September, just after Rosh Hashonah."

I agreed that it was wonderful.

"Isn't it awful about Carl?"

"What did Carl do now?"

"Didn't anyone tell you?"

No one had. And I wasn't going to ask her, either.

"How's your mother?" she asked.

"Fine," I said suspiciously. I'd been in Regina since January. Why was she asking me that?

"I'm sorry you won't get the job at Cactus Hill."

"Papa doesn't seem to know anything about Barney getting the job," I said.

"But my father is on the schoolboard, too, and he said it would be all right. We can't get married if Barney doesn't get the job."

"That's blackmail," I said.

"No, it isn't." She was close to tears. "He'll be a better teacher than you, anyway. He's not stuck-up."

"Bye," I said. "It's nice to be back."

I walked back out to the car. Papa was talking to Uncle Yacov, and he was angry: "You don't borrow another man's wife, and you don't borrow from the bank."

"Aaron, I thought I'd be able to pay it back."

"Why didn't you tell me?"

"I didn't think I'd have to. But since 1929 we've had no crop, or if we did, we haven't gotten a decent price—from over two dollars a bushel in 1928, we're down to twenty-five cents. We aren't even making enough to cover our taxes in this municipality. I had to go to the bank. If I don't pay my bills, the wholesalers will cut me off. I'll go out of business. What else could I do?"

"You should have told me."

"I couldn't, Aaron. I just couldn't."

"I'm in the machinery business, too, aren't I?"

"You only went into machinery and groceries with me because I wanted it."

"What do you want me to do?"

"The bank says they'll extend the loan if we mortgage the farm."

"The farm? Yacov, if we mortgage the farm, we could lose everything, the machinery business, the store, and the farm, too."

"What else can we do?"

"We?" Papa said. "Remember the load of seed wheat you bought that was such a great deal? You didn't even look it over, and it was infested with wild oats. Crops for miles around are paying for that. You go into these crazy ideas without thining, and it's 'we' who have to get you out of it."

They stood, locked in growing hurt.

I left them, walked up the hill, past the new barber shop, the cafe, the community hall, and the school, shiny white with red trim around the window—Barney's school, according to Tsippa—and followed the road home. I saw Barney, cheating Barney, in my school, and me without any job at all, not able to pay back the money they had spent on my year of Normal

School. I followed the road home. Saul was in the pasture breaking in horses. He was tall—six foot—and muscular, and handsome with his blue-black hair and blue eyes.

The twins were sitting on the verandah when I walked into the yard. They were eleven now, tall, grown-up girls. They weren't excited to see their big sister. Even the information that Papa had decided we might all go to the World Grain Fair in Regina in August didn't interest them. They simply chanted drily—"Well, if the crops are good . . ."

"All right, what's wrong?" I asked.

They shrugged.

"Where's Mama?"

"Upstairs crying."

"Crying? Why?"

They shrugged again.

"You're not supposed to tell Papa. The first time she cried, she made us promise not to tell him. She says he has enough to worry about."

Mama was upstairs in the twins' room scrubbing the floor. Tears were running down her cheeks.

"Mama? Mama, what's wrong?"

"I won't lose any of my children."

"Mama, we're all right."

"Disease comes in dirt," she said. "If the house isn't scrubbed every day . . . My father hasn't written to me, you know. He's mad at me. He hasn't written since Sara went away."

"Mama, I'm Sara."

"My father hasn't written to me." She hadn't seen me; she hadn't heard. "I wrote to him. Aaron mailed a letter for me every month. No one answered, not even my brothers. They're all mad at me."

"They can't be mad at you, Mama. Something must have happened."

I took the rag from her.

"Come and lie down."

I led her to the bed. Five of her brothers and sisters were dead, she said. It almost killed her mother. Her mother and father had taken the remaining living children and run away from the old country, run away from dirt and disease. Children didn't die in the New World, not from dirt. You couldn't let dirt in, or children died. Her mother scrubbed every day, and still they died. Children died.

She fell asleep. I went downstairs to make supper.

"Let's go over to the Dahls," I suggested to the twins after the supper dishes were done. "It'll cheer us up."

They shook their heads.

"Ulla's no fun any more."

"Oh," I said. "Carl again. What's he done now?"

"Nothing. He's dead."

The story spilled out. He had worked for the Dahls all winter and lived with them, but in March there had been a warm spell, so he had walked back to the tarpaper shack on his land. It was gone. Not shattered by wind. Just clean gone. Somebody had stolen it.

By then, it was getting dark and turning cold. The nearest farm was ours. By the time he arrived, his feet were frozen. He got gangrene. Ulla was with him the entire week. She was going to kill the man who had done it.

They talked about it for hours.

I went out to sit with Papa on the verandah. A full white-opal moon was rising.

"No one wrote me about Carl," I said to Papa.

"What good would it have done?"

"The twins said Ulla is going to kill the man who stole the shack."

"She'll never find him. Even if she does, Thor has hidden the gun."

"She knows how to use a knife, too."

A coyote howled, and for a few moments, the world stopped to listen.

"Papa, we're not going to lose the farm, are we?"

"Only if we mortgage it."

"I've never seen you angry at Uncle Yacov before."

"He's my baby brother. I've been taking care of him since I was seven when our mother died."

"What are you going to do?"

"I don't know."

"Why do you think Grandpa hasn't answered Mama?" I asked.

"Your grandfather is dead," he said flatly. "Your Uncle Dave wrote from Los Angeles just after you left for school last fall."

"You never told me about that, either! What's going on? I'm not a baby."

"Nothing's going on. You had your school to worry about, that's all."

"But if he's dead," I asked finally, "how can Mama think he's mad at her?"

"She doesn't know. I didn't tell her."

He stepped off the verandah and disappeared into the rustling night shadows. I sat while the white-opal moon lay irridescent mother-of-pearl over the poplars and the plum trees and the pines. Saul rode in under the mother-of-pearl light. He had been visiting across the line. Papa didn't know. She wasn't Jewish, and he didn't care, and she didn't care, and when we all met her, we wouldn't care, either. He had known all along that Mama's father had died, but Papa had made him promise not to upset the rest of us.

The next morning, I went to visit Ulla. She was hoeing the garden, and she was perfectly calm.

"Yes," she said. "I'm going to kill him. When I find him, I'm going to kill him."

"You don't mean it."

"Don't I? Do you know how you die of gangrene? Your body rots in front of your eyes; your feet, your calves, your knees, your thighs swell and turn green, and you stink of death, and you pray for death."

"Killing him won't bring Carl back."

She was silent.

"If you find him, tell Papa and he'll charge him."

"I don't want him charged. I want him dead."

I left her, perfectly calm, pulling out the weeds.

The telephone rang.

"It's not true, is it?"

It was Tsippa.

"What?"

"That you got the job."

"Tsippa, we're on the phone."

"Tell me!" There was panic in her voice. "Is it true?"

124

"I don't know."

"He's your father. Don't you talk to him? Don't you care? Papa said Barney could have the job. Why should your father run everything?"

I went to Papa.

"We're hiring a teacher," he said, "not a husband."

"But what if he doesn't marry Tsippa? They'll blame us. Uncle Yacov promised Tsippa Barney could get the job."

"Yacov makes too many promises."

We settled into hot summer, with delicate clouds laying transparent scarves against the blue, and lazy grasshopper songs rising from the grasses.

Ulla stopped in. She was on her way back from one of the farms looking for evidence, evidence that Carl had told her she would find.

"Well?" I said.

"No," she said. "But I'll find it."

She came inside with me. Mama was sitting on the verandah with her hands folded, watching the twins intently. Leah was drawing pictures, and Ruth was making up stories to go with them. Mama didn't respond to Ulla's hello.

I walked home with her.

When I came back, Mama was sitting just as I had left her, murmuring over and over, "I won't lose any of my children, I won't lose any of my children, I won't lose any of my children . . ."

I went out to find Papa.

"Papa, you have to tell Mama. It's driving her crazy. How could you do a thing like that? Why didn't you tell her?"

"I couldn't. She loves him so much, and things are so hard now. I didn't want to add to her worries."

"For God's sake, Papa, have you really looked at her? It's destroying her. You have to tell her the truth. You always told us to tell the truth. Isn't that why you were so angry at Uncle Yacov? For treating you like a child?"

"Yacov wasn't trying to protect me. He was trying to protect himself. There's a difference."

"Maybe there was in the beginning, but if you don't tell her now, it's not her you're protecting."

He came back to the verandah with me, saw her, heard her chant.

He stroked her cheek.

"Eva?"

She took his hand.

"Eva, your father isn't angry with you."

"Yes, he is. He won't answer my letters."

"He's passed away, Eva. He can't write. He's not angry. He was never angry."

"No," she said. "He isn't dead. You're trying to make me feel better. He's not dead. I haven't seen them since they left for California. Sara was just a baby. He wouldn't die before I can see them. Someday, we'll have the money, and I'll see them."

"It was an accident, Eva. He was walking home from the synagogue, and he was hit by a streetcar. He died right away."

She was angry.

"Who tells you these things?"

"Paul. Your brother. I have a letter from Los Angeles."

He brought it to her.

"This is from Chanukah. Last winter. How could a letter take so long?"

"It didn't take so long."

"How long?"

"A few months."

"You knew?" She withdrew her hand, got up from the chair, and backed away from him. "You knew, and you didn't tell me? My husband?"

She ran into the house. Papa stood, helpless, and watched her go.

The telephone rang. It was Aunt Sophie.

"What do you mean," she screamed, "by ruining Tsippa's life?"

"Aunt Sophie, for heaven's sake, we're on the telephone."

"Good. The whole world should know. The devil will eat your soul, and your children's children unto the seventh generation."

She hung up on me. Six other telephones clicked off.

I walked over to the store. She met me at the door.

"Listen. Are you listening? She's crying as if her heart would break." She waved a letter at me, then read from it: "'My heart grows cold. If your family does not think highly enough of me to hire me, then they do not think highly enough of me to welcome me into their midst.'"

"But if he really loved her—"

"And is this enough? No. Aaron won't mortgage the farm. He'll sacrifice his own brother before he'll hurt a hair on the head of that farm."

"But if we lose the farm, both of our families will starve."

"Always an answer. But answers from the head, not from the heart. A brother risks his life for his brother. And Yacov doesn't say a word. His brother Aaron couldn't be wrong. How could Aaron be wrong? God will be wrong before Aaron. Get out. Get out of my store."

I went.

I found Papa at home fixing the swather. I told him what Aunt Sophie had said.

"I love Yacov," he said tightly. "But I would be sacrificing two families for that love. I can't afford to do that."

We walked out together to sit beside the slough, shrunken by the sun in the last few years, but still jewel-blue under a summer sky. Red-winged and yellow-headed blackbirds still dipped on cattail swings, and sandpipers and bitterns still stepped with careful elegance among the reeds, and muskrats still rolled on their backs for the sheer fun of it.

"Who knows?" he said. "God willing, we'll have a good year."

Ulla called.

"I found it."

"Found what?"

"The proof. I found Carl's murderer."

"Ulla," I said. "We're on the telephone."

"I know," she said calmly. "I think everyone should know that he was murdered."

She hung up. Seven other telephones clicked off.

She was there in fifteen minutes and handed me a knife, a hunting knife, well oiled and sharpened, and wrapped in a cloth. There was a *C* carved into the bone handle.

"It was right where Carl said it would be, sitting on top of the door tucked behind the frame. And guess where I found it?"

I couldn't guess.

"At the Wilkinson's. Good old English Wilkinson who thinks he's so much better than everybody else."

"Does he know you know?"

"No. And I can't find Papa's rifle. I'll use this knife if I have to."

"No," Mama said suddenly. She had been sitting quietly beside the window. There was life in her eyes, sapphire fury. She held out her hand. "You won't. Give it to me."

Ulla drew back, put the knife in her skirt pocket.

"No. It's my job. I promised Carl."

"It's no one's job. Wilkinson's not a murderer, and neither are you. And if you think I'm going to let you ruin your life for either one of them, you have another think coming. Hand me that knife, young lady."

Ulla handed her the knife.

"Sara, tell your father to bring the car. I am going to speak to Mr. Wilkinson. Ulla, you're coming, too."

She went to get her hat.

Mr. Wilkinson was out haying. As Papa pulled the car to a stop, he got off his tractor and trudged through the thick grasses toward us.

"Good afternoon, Aaron," he said, taking off his cap. "Afternoon, Mrs. Schiller. Out for a drive?"

Papa nodded. "How's the crop?"

"Not bad. Could be a good year if the weather holds."

"Sometimes," Mama broke in, "it seems like nature is our enemy, doesn't it?"

He nodded agreeably.

"It's too bad when we have to watch out for our neighbours, too, isn't it?"

He nodded again.

She held up the knife.

"Do you know whose knife this is?"

"Could be just about anybody's. Not mine, though."

"No. Not yours. Carl's. Ulla found it in your new chicken coop. What you did when you stole Carl's shack is against the meaning of people living together in a community: life together. You ought to be—I don't know what's good enough for what you've done.

"I've been here since 1905. Twenty-eight years. In all those years, I've never known anyone to lock a door. If it was just for food, or a drink of water, or shelter from a storm, we knew nothing would be taken that wasn't needed. My mother and my father—" She faltered, began again. "My mother is alive today because her neighbours went over in thirty below weather to see why there was no smoke coming from their chimney.

"Well. You have yourself to live with. That's punishment enough."

We left him, an uncertain line against the horizon. Ulla was holding back tears.

"Now, Mr. Schiller," Mama said. "Don't you ever do anything like that to me again. It's bad enough what we have to fight in this life without the people who love us mixing in and making it worse. Since when can you save anyone from the pain of life?"

He reached for her hand. Her fingers wrapped around his.

The twins came running in with news. Papa had said we all needed a holiday. If it was all right with Mama, we would all go to Regina for the World Grain Fair. They stood, silent, insistent, eager, waiting.

"How can we afford it?" Mama asked.

"Papa said we can take food, and we have places to stay, and it will only cost gas. Please, can we go?"

"You don't have any clothes."

"We can sew. We can sew a dress for you, and a shirt for Saul. Papa said we can go to Alkali Flats and get material."

Within a few weeks they had finished their sewing: matching plaid skirts and blouses for themselves (blue to go with Ruth's eyes; orange to go with Leah's temper); a navy skirt and paisley blouse for Mama, and a surprise for me, a fitted blue voile with a full bias skirt and white organdy collar and cuffs. Saul had earned his new catalogue shirt and pants by his work on the farm.

"You are in charge of us kids," the twins informed me

matter-of-factly, "and all of us kids are going to sleep in tents. There are going to be tents just for us."

"There are? How many of 'us kids' are there?"

"Thirty."

"How come nobody told me?"

"Papa says you already know."

"Oh," Papa said, when I complained, "I thought I told you."

The municipal council—Dr. Lowe, Mr. Dahl, Mr. Wilkinson, Papa, and Uncle Yacov—had decided that the taxes our municipality was able to collect, what little there was, would go for the school and the children: gas would be paid for to drive the children to Regina; tents had been arranged for us to sleep in on the exhibition grounds; food would be sent in by the parents.

"Does that mean I have the job?" I asked.

"Yes," he said, "but it wasn't my decision. I left it up to the rest of the board, and it was unanimous. Even your Uncle Yacov voted for you."

I was so excited that I almost telephoned Ulla to give her the good news.

We drove out of our rolling hills onto the flat into an endless world of sky, with our heads right up in the sky, up in the blue and the light. We could see the world for miles and miles, right to its edge, and the world could see us.

We rode in the sky for hours, and then we saw Regina, a rough edge on the thin line of the horizon at first, and then a cluster of buildings growing up around the white marble legislative building. Thirty children, shy, scrubbed clean, sitting on top of their bedding, awaited me.

For three days we lived in circus magic. We went for breakfast with the Fat Lady and the Thin Man; we settled the Siamese twins' argument about whether to turn left or right; we splashed the elephant, and he splashed us. We looked at exhibits of dusky golden kernels of wheat, of shiny flat brown flax, fluffy angel food cakes, sparkling rose-hip preserves, photographs, crocheting, quilting. . . . We saw shows of dainty golden Jersey cows, sure-footed Clydesdales. . . . We ate candy floss, and candied apples, and hot dogs, and ice-cream. We rode on the magical horses of the carousel, up and down, round and round, up and down, round and round; on the ferris wheel, into the world and out of it, into the world and out of it . . .

And on the very last night we saw flowers in the sky, great pink and blue and red and silver blossoms bursting into bloom above our heads.

The next morning we waited to go home with tousled hair, rumpled clothes, and the sparkle of a thousand stories in our eyes.

There was a grey cloud overhead as we left Regina behind, a thin line on the horizon once again. Mama laughed with delight. Clouds were a good omen.

We were on the flat, driving past abandoned homes when the cloud caught up with us. Something dropped on the windshield. Rain? Hail?

Grasshoppers.

We watched as the cloud passed overhead, flew south ahead of us.

By the time we reached Short Haul, the fields had been stripped, the ripening green-gold grain only ragged stalks. We drove into the yard, and the grasshoppers crunched underfoot.

11

A Difference to the Horizon

Saul was outside waiting with the horses to drive us to school, and Leah and I were waiting at the door. Ruth was playing with her cat.

"Ruth!" I said. "We'll be late!"

"Leave her alone!" Mama snapped. "It isn't good to hurry breakfast."

"Mama, she hasn't even started breakfast!"

Then, suddenly, I was in my classroom, and as I began to speak, the students rose with one graceful motion and floated out of their desks, through the ceiling, out over the hills. Inkwell eyes on five rows of wooden desks accused. A tall grey man with stooped shoulders stood in the doorway. He was disappointed.

I woke up.

The next morning, Saul, Leah, and I were waiting while Ruth played with her cat.

"Mama," I said. "I'm the teacher. I can't be late. Make her hurry up."

"Leave her alone!"

It was my dream. I grabbed my lunch and walked.

The students weren't silent and watching at all. They were

running all over the yard in the amber light of a September morning getting their first-day-of-school clothes scruffy. We walked into the school together, up the steps, through the cloakroom, into our classroom, a mint-green room with a blackboard, a map of the world, and five rows of little wooden desks, smaller desks near the register, big desks near the windows, a whole wall of windows, our farm in the distance to the west. I could see the roof of the barn above the trees.

Thirty children sat, expectant, trusting, behind those inkwell eyes. I didn't know what to do. Which grade would I work with first? What would the other grades do while I was working with one?

"Teacher?"

It was Amy with a serious little face and straw-blond braids and tears in her eyes.

"Gunnar didn't believe me about the fireworks."

Ah! That was it. We would talk about our summer, and then we would write about it, and while the older grades were writing, the grade ones and twos and I would write together, and then we would use the story to learn reading. After that, we would all go on a field trip to the pasture across the tracks and collect late summer flowers and come back to class to name them and press them . . . and then it would be time to go home.

Leah and Ruth walked in.

"We're sorry we're late, Miss Schiller," Leah said.

Ruth said nothing.

Suddenly, Papa appeared at the door. There was a problem with the senior room. Mr. Gallagher, the principal, had only sixteen students; if the quota of eighteen were not filled, it would have to be closed. He walked in and tapped Leah and Ruth on their shoulders. They picked up their books.

"Good-bye, Miss Schiller," Ruth said.

At three o'clock, like dandelion down wafted over the prairie, the class was gone. I sat for the first time that day and took off my shoes.

There was a *Register* in my desk.

What was a *Register* for? No one had mentioned a register at Normal School. How would I get through the year? Is that what a born teacher was? Someone who knew instinctively at

133

what age and stage a child was ready for join-up writing, or long division, or the mountains and rivers of Canada?

"I think it's time we met."

The man holding out his hand to me wasn't grey or stooped or disappointed. He was about my age, and he was smiling.

"I'm Sean Gallagher, your principal. How was your first day?"

"Inspired," I said. "But with no books and no curriculum, I don't know if I can be inspired every day."

"No books?" He looked puzzled. And then embarrassed. He had forgotten.

In his classroom, the senior room, was a wooden cupboard with a complete set of *High Roads to Reading* for each of my seven grades, Professor Quance's *Speller* with lists of spelling words for each grade, and a curriculum. Grade three was supposed to learn Japan. I didn't know anything about Japan except that they had cherry blossoms and kimonos and that Canada was selling them scrap steel. How was I supposed to teach Japan?

"Whoa! Hold your horses," Mr. Gallagher said. "The curriculum is new. They haven't written the books to fit it yet. But even if the books for the students aren't ready, there is a set of books which outlines what we're supposed to teach. If you'd like, I can order them for you."

"Would I!"

For now, at least, I had reading and spelling; I could give them work to place them in arithmetic; I had Professor Anderson's book from Normal School on simple experiments that could be done with materials from around the home. . . . We could do one of those, maybe the one with the candle and the shoebox that showed that light travelled in straight lines.

By the time I had finished worrying and planning, it was seven o'clock. I walked home with my head up in liquid sky colours.

The next morning, once again, we waited while Ruth played with her cat. "Mama!" I began, and, "Sara," Mama said. "She's only a baby." I walked. Leah waited for her twin. Saul waited with the horses to drive them the mile to school. He winked as I passed him.

It was a terrible day. No matter what we were doing—

spelling, reading, or arithmetic—somebody was always "finished." I'd leave whichever grade I was working with to check the "finished" hand—and the child hadn't understood in the first place. Mr. Gallagher thought it was funny. The only things he didn't think were funny were the two carrot-topped little boys, Ray and Roy, identical twins whom the other children teased and poked and tormented into indignant reaction, and then turned to me to advise solemnly, "Beat them, Teacher, beat them. The other teacher always beat them."

Day three was also terrible. The children only understood personal nose-to-nose explanations; Ray and Roy couldn't sit still for even three minutes; and the other children continually urged beatings. When I asked if the other teacher had beat them, too, they said yes. When I asked if it had helped them learn, they said no: it had helped them learn worse. I guessed, then, that there was no point in beating anyone.

But Ray and Roy still held up their hands to ward off blows, and the other children still did their best to get them into trouble, and I didn't know what I was going to do with children who understood only beatings.

"How come your sisters got to go to grade eight, and I didn't?"

It was Gunnar, tall, gangly Gunnar, who didn't believe in fireworks and who had barely passed grade six the year before. I set the other children learning their arithmetic facts on the board and went to talk to him.

"Grade eight is very hard," I said. "If you go to grade eight, you'll probably fail, but if you stay in grade seven, you will do a good job of it and pass."

"How come it's not hard for them? They're girls."

"Oh. Well. Girls," I said. "Girls don't have to stay home and help with the harvest. They can come to school more, and they have more time to think about school."

"I think sometimes," he said.

"No, I mean, Leah and Ruth have more time to do their homework, and they don't have to miss school. Helping with the harvest is very important, and you're smart, so if you stay in grade seven, you can do both. You can help and still pass."

At recess, he informed Leah and Ruth that they went into

135

grade eight because they were dumb. Then he went out and hit three home runs.

When I got home, Ulla was setting the table. She had come over to talk to Mama, and she was staying for supper.

"Ulla's getting married," Mama announced accusingly.

"Already? Who?"

"Otto. From across the line," Ulla said, smiling a pretty, shy smile. "What do you think?"

"I think . . . you'll be very happy."

"Of course, she'll be happy," Mama said. "He loves her. And Ulla will love him. Real love doesn't happen like in *Ladies Home Journal*. You have to be sensible. It takes time."

"You weren't. All Papa had when you married him were his dreams."

"I had faith in your father. Ulla has faith in Otto."

"You loved Papa. Ulla doesn't love Otto."

"I will, though," Ulla said.

We talked about it all through supper. He was like her father, blond, blue-eyed, strong as an ox, and gentle as a lamb—and there was a gentle and contented delight in her that I couldn't remember ever seeing.

The next evening, I sat at my desk watching the sunset colours shape and form. I had had a headache since morning. I had tried to teach Ray and Roy simple mathematical concepts using pencils and notebooks: "Amy gave me one pencil, and Gunnar gave me one. How many pencils do I have now?" "Two, Teacher." "Then one and one must be two. Oscar gave me one notebook, and Hans gave me one. How many notebooks am I holding?" "Two, Teacher." "How much is one and one?"

They didn't know.

I would leave to answer a raised hand, instructing the twins to tell me the answer when I came back. On my return, there would be a whispered, "Hey, Gunnar, what's one and one?" and Gunnar's response: "Five."

My headache wasn't getting better.

Mr. Gallagher offered to drive me home. Mama was waiting with her arms folded when I walked in. "You should have married Meyer. God knows who you'll find to marry you now."

"Oh, for heaven's sake," I said.

"He's a handsome man," she said, "and he's not Jewish. Be careful."

"He's my principal," I said.

"Did he kiss you?" Leah and Ruth chorussed. "Did Mr. Gallagher kiss you?"

"The last teacher was his girlfriend," Mama said.

"She used the strap all the time," Leah added. "She was awful."

My dream that night was a mixture of eyes: disapproval in Mama's, eager questioning in the children's, and disappointment in a tired, stooped school inspector.

The next morning the children were terrible.

I'd hear an indignant "Hey!" and one of the carrot-topped little boys was out of his seat while the culprits sat demurely, eyes downcast.

"The next time I hear a peep out of one of you!" I finally exploded. "You see that? I'm writing your names across the top of the board, and putting 100 percent below, and with each squeak, you go down five marks. And the next time one of you pokes the twins, you get Importunate—a big fat I—on your report card."

There was shocked silence. Even Gunnar was at attention. Amy had tears in her eyes.

Mr. Gallagher was impressed.

But terror wouldn't work forever.

The next day, as a reward for our good behaviour, we took our lunch out to the big rock in the pasture. Ray and Roy, attention span of mosquitoes and feet like wings, got there first. Gunnar was second. He was calling the twins liars and they were objecting.

"Teacher," Gunnar defended himself, "they said Mr. Gallagher said the world is round."

"It is," I said.

"Then how come," he said, "when we get to the top of the hill, we don't fall off?"

"You're right," I agreed. "We should fall off."

"And if it's round," he continued, "why don't the birds just fly away forever?"

The other children were nodding agreeably.

"I think," I said, "it's something called gravity. The earth is so big that it attracts everything to it." I dropped a shoe. "See? It falls right back to the earth, like a magnet."

"What's a magnet?" he asked.

Amy, plaits swinging, came running up with a stone scraper she had just found, and the subject changed to the Indian children who used to play where we were playing and the buffalo that used to scratch their coats in the spring on the very rock we were sitting on, this very buffalo wallow, wearing down the earth in a circle as they walked around it.

"Where did they all go?" Amy asked.

"Who?" I asked.

"The buffalo and the children like us."

"Well . . ." I started, "when our parents and grandparents came with fences and ploughs, some moved away, and others—well—just died. Like when your father ploughs a field and the prairie dogs have nowhere to go."

Then Gunnar remembered Constable Yeaman telling him that the Americans had given the dead soldiers' contaminated blankets to the Indians so that they would catch smallpox and die, too. With the worries of falling off the earth and killing buffalo and Indians—not to mention the dreaded *I*—it was a gloomy day. Mr. Gallagher thought that was funny, too.

"Where am I going to get information about gravity and magnets?" I demanded. "They'll probably ask about flying next."

"From me," he said. "I have a bachelor of science. I was going into medicine before the depression hit."

"You were?"

"I were. Next time I go home to Saskatoon, I'll bring back some of my material from university."

"What about right now? What about gravity? What about not falling off the earth? At least once a week, I dream about the school inspector coming right in the middle of my worst lesson, and me not knowing anything, and the twins still can't add, and it's all true."

"You're taking life too seriously, Miss Schiller. How about coming with me to play bridge with the station agent and his wife sometime?"

"What about your girlfriend?"

"Hester and I used to play with them all the time. She won't mind. It's natural that we be friends."

"Is it?"

"Of course. We're teaching together."

"Oh," I said.

He drove me home. I invited him in for supper.

"Tell me, Mr. Gallagher," Mama said graciously, "are you and Miss Dougherty planning to marry?"

They weren't. He was Protestant Irish, and she was Catholic, and his parents would never live through it. "Your parents know what's best for you," Mama said.

"Mama," I said after he had left, "how could you ask him something so personal?"

"I'm your mother," she said.

"If there's gravity," Gunnar asked me first thing in the morning, "how come birds can fly and flies don't just crawl around?"

"That's a good question, Gunnar. But the problem isn't gravity, it's how birds and flies and airplanes fly. You'll notice, though, that they all come back to earth. They are attracted back to the magnet, the earth."

"What's a magnet?" he asked.

That night, I woke up in a panic out of a dream that was a mixture of Mama's anger, the children's confusion, and the superintendent's disappointment: I couldn't explain a magnet.

When I got up, Papa was making breakfast. He sent me in to Mama. She was sitting up in bed, her eyes a fevered and frightened blue.

"Sara, I had a dream. My mother is very sick. You have to go. She has to see at least one of my children before she dies."

"But she doesn't even know us, and she hasn't seen you for twenty years. You're the one who should go."

"Don't argue with me. It has to be one of you. You're the reason she left the old country, after all."

I didn't understand.

"Don't argue with me! Promise!"

"But, Mama, it will take the rest of my salary for the year. I won't be able to help you and Papa out."

"Promise me!"

I promised. I brushed her hair back from her forehead—
silver white and long again—and I promised.

When I got to school, the yard was strangely empty, the
classroom strangely silent. My students, from the tiniest grade
one to the gangliest grade seven, stood in a menacing circle.
Three teen-age boys, tall, thin, with gentle eyes, were trapped
in their midst. As I appeared at the door, the culprits scattered
to their desks. I asked the three what was wrong. They didn't
understand. I asked their names. They shook their heads. Gunnar spoke to them in Norwegian, Oscar in Russian, Hans in German . . . They spoke Yiddish. Their names were Moishe,
Chaim, and Yisroel. Gunnar snickered. Shadows of fear
flickered across their eyes. I glared at him. I glared at all of them.
"Remember the *I*?" I said, pointing threateningly to the chart.
"Remember getting zero on your next test? I'm going to speak
to the boys in Yiddish. I'm going to tell them that from now
on, I will speak to them in English because they will get used
to the sound of the language faster. I'm going to tell them that
almost every one of you started out speaking another language,
and look how confident and rotten you are now. And if there
is a peep out of any one of you, you will *all* get zero.
Understand?"

Between guarding the three boys, keeping an eye on Ray
and Roy, and answering "finished," by the time Mr. Gallagher
appeared at the door at three o'clock, I was close to tears.

"It's the first-year jitters, for sure," he said cheerfully.

"No, it's not," I snapped. "It's three new students who don't
speak a word of English."

"Whoa. Hold your horses. Three new students?"

"You're the principal. You're supposed to know what goes
on in your school. If they'd been Irish or Scottish or English
or German or almost anything except Jewish, it wouldn't have
taken their father nine years to get them into the country, and
I wouldn't have this problem. They'd be in the senior room
speaking English like they should be."

"Now, now, Miss Schiller. You exaggerate, surely. Was it not
just the other week that you informed me that the Chinese and
East Indians do not even gain entrance to the door of our fair
land?"

"What about it?"

"Be grateful for small mercies."

"When mercies are that small, it's hard to be grateful. If I could at least speak Yiddish to them, it wouldn't be so bad, but how would the other kids feel? Nobody speaks German or Russian or Norwegian or Swedish to them. How am I going to teach English to these three and seven other grades seven subjects each?"

He didn't think it was funny, but he didn't have any ideas, either, except to look at the lighter side of life. The station agent and his wife were most anxious to play bridge. I informed him that he was Irish Protestant, and that he had a girlfriend, and that my mother didn't approve.

"I'm your principal," he said. "It's natural that we'd be friends."

Papa was cooking supper when I got home.

"I hate it when Mama is sick," Ruth said. "All Papa knows how to cook is *mamaliga* and cottage cheese."

"Why don't you cook?" I snapped. "I've been washing floors since I was seven. I bet you two can't even hold a broom—let alone get ready for school on time."

"We're the youngest," she said. "We don't have to."

Papa raised an eyebrow at her, and she disappeared.

"Am I still supposed to go to Los Angeles?" I asked.

He nodded.

Meyer was in Los Angeles.

There were new eyes in my dream that night. They were Meyer's.

The next morning, Mama was still in bed, and, for the first time—just to spite me, no doubt—Ruth was ready, and Saul drove us all to school. I caught my students happily tormenting the three boys.

"Red-handed," I said.

"Are we going to get zero?" they asked.

"Worse than that," I said.

I marched them into the classroom, and thirty pairs of eyes watched as under each of their names, I placed an accusing fat *I*. They were miserable. At the end of the morning, I relented.

"I'll make you a deal," I said.

They were listening.

"If you help Chaim and Moishe and Yisroel learn English, I'll take back the *I*'s."

We listed nouns that were important to us—cold, snow, horse, school, ship, sun, milk—and put the translations for all of them in our languages beside them. The next day, we would add adjectives to the list—thin ice, gentle horse, light snow, warm sun—the following day, verbs, and the day after that, adverbs. Each day, before we added to our new list, we would have a spelling test for the older children, a reading test for the younger children, and a vocabulary test for the three boys.

When I got home, the twins were making their favourite supper: potatoes and eggs fried in butter with dill pickles and canned crabapples and whipped cream. Dr. Lowe was with Mama. She was still in pain, still nauseated, still feverish, and still insistent that I go to Los Angeles. After supper, we all played Monopoly, even Papa who hated it because it was exactly what banks were doing to people.

When we went to bed that night, the twins promised God that if Mama got better and didn't have to have an operation, they would never fight or be lazy again.

The three boys were learning their vocabulary, but the other children were laughing at their accents.

"Do you like it when someone laughs at you?" I asked.

They didn't: they wanted to kick those people in the head, hit them in the gut.

"Then don't you think you should tell the boys you're sorry?"

No, they said sensibly: Moishe and Chaim and Yisroel didn't know "I'm sorry" in English.

"You can say it in Yiddish. I said. "*Ich bin shuldig.* It might be nice if you tried to learn a few words of their language, too."

"Really?" they said.

"Really."

"Aw, shucks," they said.

My Norwegian and Swedish and German and Russian and English children learned "I'm sorry—*Ich bin shuldig.*"

But the three boys still had their accents.

The day Papa left with Mama for her operation in Regina

was a bright, still December day, the kind of day when smoke rises from the chimneys as clearly defined against the blue as a white scarf on a dark head. I went down to the train station to say good-bye accompanied by the children, bright bits of colour on the white hill, as important to the landscape as the burgundy elevators and the black railroad ribbons tracing the line of the coulee behind it. Papa helped Mama onto the train and the black steam engine chuffed away from us to wind between brilliant hills. White steam clouds hung in puffs in the blue.

That night, after the boys had done the chores and the twins had cleaned up, we lay on Mama and Papa's bed and imagined our favourite things for the rest of us to guess: the cat curled into your neck, Mama telling stories, the gas lamp through the window when you were coming in from the barn . . . Then we had to guess our favourite pictures of each other: Saul's gentleness with the horses and patience with everyone; Ruth staying up all night to nurse her cat. There were blazing northern lights that night, sea-green and indigo and oriental red moving in a slow dance across the sky: souls dancing, Leah said, spirits hovering above the earth protecting us.

Sometimes, it seemed to me, the spirits didn't do a very good job.

I went with Sean one night, finally, to see the lighter side of life at the bridge table. It was fun. Sean and I lost. I didn't care until Mrs. Station Agent said that Sean and Hester always used to win. All of a sudden, I didn't like her or her egg-salad sandwiches.

When I got home, my two little sisters were waiting up to find out if Mr. Gallagher had kissed me. "Don't be silly," I said. "He's my principal." They believed me.

Mama was right. He was handsome. He had rich wavy black hair and smiling Irish eyes, and he invited himself over on the weekends to cheer us up. On Saturdays we played Monopoly, while he and Saul told jokes about depression rabbits that were so thin and tired and slow that when you were out hunting, you'd run right past them, and they ended up chasing you. On Sundays we listened to Eddie Cantor and Fred Allen and Jack Benny on the radio.

Otto and Ulla were married on a night when a light glittery

snow was falling, a light glittery snow made silver sparkles by a faint and distant moon. She wore a blue wool suit that brought out the summer sunshine in both their eyes.

"Jeepers," Ruth said on the way home. "I bet if you'd married Meyer, you'd have a baby by now, and we'd be aunts."

"What good would it do you? I'd be in Los Angeles, remember? You'd never see me again. That's what happened to Mama."

"Will Mama be all right?" she asked.

"Yes," I said, and as I said it, I knew that it was true.

And then it was the winter holiday, with Sean at home in Saskatoon, and the school empty and cold, and the four of us at home playing Monopoly and snakes and ladders and listening to the radio. Papa was staying with Mama in Regina until he was sure she was all right.

My principal was standing at my desk.

"How was your holiday?" I asked.

"Boring," he snapped.

"Too bad," I said. "It was pretty exciting here. Two pregnancies, two births, no deaths, and Aunt Sophie is sending Tsippa to Winnipeg to find a husband. How's Hester?"

"Why didn't you answer my letter?"

"What letter?"

"The one I gave Tsippa when she was in Saskatoon over the holiday."

"Why would you give Tsippa a letter for me? You know she and I hate each other."

"I didn't believe it."

"I didn't get the letter, did I?"

"Did you miss me?"

"Yes."

A smile broke into his Irish eyes, and he perched on the edge of my desk. "The teachers' convention is coming up in a month or so. We could have a wicked weekend together."

"Mr. Gallagher! Such talk! You're lucky you're not Jewish. You'd have to marry me."

"You could convert," he said. "We're accepting Irish converts this week. After that, becoming a Protestant would be as easy as falling off a log."

We laughed. We laughed till our sides hurt. It wasn't funny.

Ulla was home for a visit. She was calm, quiet, and beaming: she had thrown up ten days in a row.

"Would you marry Sean?" she asked.

"His parents wouldn't let him marry a Catholic, even though she's Irish. Can you imagine them letting him marry a Jew?"

"Would you marry a Christian?"

"If I could have Jewish children. Otherwise, there's too much danger of children coming home from church ashamed of their Jewish parent. Of course, Mama can hardly wait for me to get married. Now that Meyer's gone, she thinks I'm doomed. She says she's aged twenty years over it."

"Poor Sara," she said.

I thought she was going to cry. I thought I was going to cry.

"For heaven's sake, Ulla, stop that. You used to be tough as nails. I don't think getting married was good for you."

"Oh, yes, it was," she said with a mischievous smile, "and it will be good for you, too."

In my dream that night the whole school was singing to Ulla and Otto and their new baby in clear accentless voices: "Can you bake an apple pie, Billy Boy, Billy Boy? Can you bake an apple pie, charming Billy . . ."

I woke up singing.

"What's wrong with you?" Ruth asked.

"I figured out how to eradicate accents from the face of Saskatchewan," I said.

That morning I walked into the classroom, threw open the windows, and we did music for an hour: "Can you bake an apple pie, Billy Boy, Billy Boy? Can you bake an apple pie, Charming Billy . . ." We practised the pronunciation of the words—Kann yooo baake ann aaple pii—veree slo-owlee and cleerlee for at least half an hour. We practised stress, the first syllable on Billy and apple, practised intonation, raising our voices at the end of a question. We did music to cheer us up, and music as a reward. Sometimes, for the fun of it, we practised stress and pronunciation and intonation with our new vocabulary and our reading stories, and, one day, we noticed that no one was teasing the boys because we were all talking the same. The *I*'s came down. When Sean asked what was going on, I said it was the answer to a dream.

I was making a diagram of the planets moving around the sun. We were going to talk about what life might be like on Mars. I was looking forward to discussing it with Gunnar.

"*Níl béarla agam.*"

My heart sank.

"I no speak—" it was Sean—"the English, Miss."

"You've come to the right place."

"Good," he said. He moved closer. "Me like teacher."

"You're not going to kiss me, are you?" I moved behind my desk. He followed. "Not in my own classroom."

"Yes. Me principal. You take orders."

He caught me.

I was beginning to like the lighter side of life.

Mama was coming home, and the twins were happily fighting again. The teachers' convention was coming up. I was looking forward to it. It would be a holiday. It was only natural that Sean and I would go together.

From the moment I stepped into his car, for one complete hour through the March cold, past frozen sloughs and dust-filled ditches, he was unnaturally silent. When we pulled up at the hotel, he got out, slammed the door, and disappeared.

Angela and Lilly were waiting for me in the lobby. Angela was still fluffy-haired and blue-eyed, but she looked tired instead of angelic. Lilly was wearing a new dress, and there was a proud lift to her head.

"Lilly's in love," Angela announced.

"Really? Who?" I asked.

"A farmer from around my school," Lilly said.

"A farmer's wife," Angela teased. "Work, work, work all day."

"It's not so bad," I said.

"I'll love living on the farm again," Lilly said.

"Then you must know something I don't," Angela said. "Come on, Schiller. Spill. We saw you drive up with him. Are you in love? Are you going to marry him?"

"Don't be silly. He was almost engaged to last year's teacher. I'm this year's."

"Oh, oh," Angela said.

"I'm not upset," I said. "I'm realistic."

146

"Okay," she said.

Lilly and I turned on her.

"What about you?"

"You know me. Here today, gone tomorrow. Come on. I told the Avon lady you were coming."

As we walked through the lobby past the restaurant, I saw Sean talking to a woman with short curly hair and a turned-up nose. She was crying.

I bought a lipstick and nailpolish.

I didn't see my principal for the rest of the day. I didn't see him until the next morning when our inspector, faded blond, stooped, and enthusiastic, was giving his paper on phonics. Teaching phonics was out of fashion, he said, but it was practical, and it worked, and who cared about fashion. If a child knew the rules—which letter combinations made which sounds—then he was independent and could figure out new words on his own. Knowing that the *e* at the end of the word made the interior vowel long—*a* in *hat* becomes *a* in *hate* let the child know what to do when he met a word like *gate* or *mate*.

That evening I saw both of them: Sean, my principal who had kissed me in my classroom, and her, the dark-haired cutie. He had kissed *her* in my classroom, too, no doubt. They were dancing. She wasn't crying.

I wasn't, either.

"Cheer up, Schiller," Angela said. "He's not good-looking, anyway. Let's go get drunk."

"Teachers don't get drunk," I said. "They lose their jobs."

"Not if they don't get caught, they don't. Come on, you two."

We went.

The next morning, he was waiting to drive me back.

"Your car is too cold," I said. "The atmosphere is unfriendly. Life is too short. A stitch in time saves nine. Look before you leap. If at first you don't succeed, give up. I'll find another lift, thank you."

That Monday afternoon I looked up and there he was—tall, stooped, faded blond, and enthusiastic. It was two o'clock. We were right in the middle of our art lesson, looking out the

147

window and talking about how big things looked when you were close to them, and how small they looked from far away. We were just about to look at each other's pictures and say what we saw.

"Now isn't that fine! What might this be?" the inspector was asking, walking up and down the rows and stopping at each desk in turn.

"The sky," one of the carrot-topped twins said of his blue page.

"A picture," Gunnar said of his buffalo wallow in a coneflower-filled pasture.

"The world," Amy said of her horizon and sky.

"Canada," Moishe said of his red elevator on white hills.

While the inspector walked and admired, an image of my art teacher floated across my eyes commenting sadly, "There have been teachers who have taught art knowing as little as you do."

Then he was at the front of the room with the *Register* in his hand, calling the students by name and asking questions. Ray and Roy watched him with fascinated shining eyes and didn't flit out of their desks to turn up under his elbow more than once.

Our next and last lesson for the day was music, the time when I opened the windows, and we breathed deeply, and sang our little hearts out.

"Correct me if I'm wrong, Miss Schiller," he said as he was leaving, "but didn't Billy Boy eat cherry pie?"

"Yes," I said. "But none of us ever has."

"And the *I* you have on the chart. What does that stand for?"

"Importunate," I said. "Insubordinate. Inconsiderate. Impossible."

"Oh," he said, pleased. "They understand vocabulary like that?"

"No," I said. "They don't. They just know it must be terrible to be all that. That's probably why it works so well."

"Oh," he said. "I see."

I watched his car wind along the road to our farm, just as I had dreamed. He would go in to Papa, shaking his head sadly—

I didn't want to think about it.

I was putting art work up on the wall when Sean came in.

"How was it?"

"Fine," I snapped.

"Oh," he said.

He didn't leave.

"What were you doing?"

"Art," I snapped again.

"Why didn't you switch to literature? That's your best subject."

"Because I didn't think of it. And the kids aren't stupid."

"You're right. They aren't. They would do the same thing if they were you."

"Thanks for the information," I said.

"Your father actually believes that the inspector knows all the children in the district by name because of his trick of calling them by name—with the *Register* in his hand, of course," Mr. Gallagher continued. "He goes by the children's eyes when he asks them questions. If they light up, he knows the teacher has the subject in hand."

"Mr. Gallagher," I said, "is this what is so charmingly referred to as 'Irish blarney?'"

He perched on the corner of my desk with his impish Irish grin.

"The station agent has invited us over for a game. I was wondering what you might be thinking of that?"

"I might be thinking it would be unnatural. Especially," I lied, "since I'm going to Los Angeles this summer to see another man."

"Oh," he said. "Would it now."

I walked home following a pink snow road through pink snow hills under pink evening light. Papa was hearing right this minute that his daughter, too, like so many of the previous teachers, was below par: "I don't blame your daughter," the inspector was saying. "There are no supplies, and the schools are ungraded. When I walk into one of our rural schools, I just slide my standards down a notch or two."

By the time I turned off the road into the shadows of our trees, the inspector's car was gone.

"That's my daughter," Papa said as I walked in. "A teacher who makes the students' eyes light up."

I cried. My father held me, and I cried.

Gunnar passed grade seven; Ray and Roy didn't learn what one and one meant; Chaim, Moishe, and Yisroel were all ready for grade six; Amy drew lovely pictures of the world, with perspective if she felt like it; and Mama was home well. Sean and I shook hands and wished each other a good summer. I was lying.

The next morning, Mama looked me over in my white wool suit and pink silk blouse, nodded with satisfaction, and told me to live my own life. I couldn't believe it was me, couldn't believe I was actually the one Papa was taking to the train, I who would be waving good-bye, off to see the world. We drove past Cactus Hill School, through Short Haul, wound out of our green summer hills onto the flat to Weyburn, a city the size of Estevan, but with one hill and a slow-moving brown river instead of a valley, and an asylum instead of a coal mine.

We drove down the hill, crossed the river, pulled up at the train station in our own little cloud of dust, and walked out of the bright sunshine into a long room of dark wood and tobacco smells. A ticket agent emerged out of the gloom in a green visor cap to dispense tickets with no smile, no conversation, as if he had nothing to do with sending people out into the world, nothing to do with boxes and bundles, hushed expectation, and nervous, tearful good-byes.

The train chugged, whistled, hissed to a stop, and I was on it, chuffing away into the west: Papa, the station, the hill, became dots on the flat—and disappeared.

There was a tap on my shoulder. I turned to a waiting hand at the end of a uniform.

"Ticket, please."

He said it like he was announcing his own funeral. I gave him the ticket. I smiled.

"We do not smile on the CPR, madame," he said. He took my ticket and moved on.

"I'd report him," a voice chirped from behind. I turned

around. She was about my age, perfectly marcelled and manicured in a white linen suit. There was a fur coat and a
cherub-like little girl on the seat beside her.

"He was being smart," she continued cheerfully. "He's the
first black conductor I've seen, and I wouldn't be surprised
if he's the last."

The cherub, chestnut curled and blue-eyed, had climbed
down from her seat and was climbing into mine.

"I hope you're not afraid of children," the Mommie said.

I said I wasn't.

We were rolling through the world my mother wanted me
to see clearly, my world, the world of big sky and low land.
Women stopped, an arm upraised to a clothesline, a hand
outstretched to a child. We crossed the line of their horizon
and disappeared.

I would have a whole summer to myself. I'd visit ocean and
palm trees, cities and deserts, cousins and uncles I'd never met
and a grandmother I didn't remember. I'd be away from the
hurt of Sean. I'd see Meyer. I got a lump in my throat when I
thought about Meyer. I'd missed his laughter and his warmth,
his friendship and his love. And what had I achieved here that
any one of the three hundred and two graduates of Normal
School—except for Barney, of course—couldn't have? Maybe
I should have married Meyer. Maybe I still could. There were,
after all, other children and other places where I could teach.

I thanked Mama for forcing me to go.

"It's so dreary," the marcelled Mommie said from behind
my shoulder.

"Dreary?" I said.

"Nothing to look at. I don't know how anyone can live here.
What does one do in such desolation?"

"Desolation?"

"Look at it," she said. "Nothing. Not a building or a tree
for miles."

"What about the sky?"

"It gives me the creeps. Where I live, you never have to look
at the sky at all."

She was from Hamilton. They were in shipbuilding. She
didn't imagine, from what she was seeing, that there was any
society here at all. Her sister was married to the lieutenant

151

governor of British Columbia, and there was barely even any society there.

We snaked into Moose Jaw, a disorganized city set in scrubby hills. Moose Jaw was the end of the rum-running line. I walked up and down the platform looking for Chicago gangsters. There weren't any. Although one man did come up and ask Mommie if she wanted to sell her child. We got back on the train.

The child—she said her name was Ellen Ann—fell asleep on my lap. Mommie went out to the lounge car to have a cigarette. We chugged across the land into aquamarine skies laced with cinnamon and gold.

The conductor—the black conductor—was back with the grave announcement that my berth was ready. He was handsome, a bit like Janine, except that his skin was a mocha glow instead of cream. He introduced himself. He was Ethelbert D. J. Bartholemew of Edinburgh, Scotland. The madame with the child had been quite correct: black men were allowed to serve dinner and make beds, but they were not allowed to take tickets. He was the porter, merely helping out a fellow Scot who was ill.

"Fellow Scot?" I said.

"Aye," he said gravely. "You are no more surprised than the good Scots themselves, especially the good Scots of British Columbia."

"But you don't have an accent," I said.

"Neither, madame," he said, "do you."

I climbed into my berth, wriggled out of my clothes, and into my nightgown. The world went by as I was rocked to sleep.

At six the next morning, I was dressed and sitting in the daycoach waiting for the Rocky Mountains.

"Och," Mr. Bartholemew said. "You didna' learn your geography, lass. You'll noo be having your first peek of a peak before the sun is well overhead."

Suddenly, he was very Scottish. He said it came and went.

At ten o'clock, there they were, the Three Sisters in the misted blue distance, shining white peaks, white meringue peaks, a fork lifted and the white meringue caught, frozen, formed out of the breath of the blue. I wanted to push the mountains back, to let the sky and the light in: there was a battle between the earth and the heavens, and the heavens were losing.

Mommie and the child were back. Ellen Ann scrambled into my lap. Mommie sat down with relief. She had changed into a black silk suit.

"It's so wearing being with a child all day."

I agreed.

"I should have brought one of the maids."

I agreed with that, too.

"Do you have any children? You're very good with them."

I said I was a teacher.

"Isn't Ellen Ann lucky! We'll be together all the way to Vancouver."

We were climbing into the mountains, into a world formed out of anger, thrusting rock, lurking pine, and malevolent white peaks that swallowed up most of the sky. The prairie, once a lake bottom, was born out of a dream of water.

Mommie didn't like the Rocky Mountains any more than I did. The Ontario hills, she assured me, I would love: they were gentle, nothing at all like this.

"The Ontario hills," Mr. Bartholemew announced, "have people from Ontario on them, English colonizers who grind wherever they go. These mountains are untamed—a wild, natural beauty. Excuse me. I have a train to tend to."

"How he has kept his job is beyond me," Mommie fumed at his retreating back. "I'll report him. I certainly will. My brother-in-law will see to it."

"He's just trying to get your goat," I said.

Ellen Ann and I left Mommie fuming and went out to experience the mountains from the observation car with the scent of pine in the wind, the cinders flying back, and the mountains frowning down. When we found her in the lounge car, Mommie was still fuming. Ethelbert D. J. Bartholemew's voice floated ahead of him into the car: "Great Divide, seventh wonder of the world, coming up!"

"There, you see? There he goes again, shouting like that, scaring people half to death. I don't believe he knows a thing he's talking about. 'Great Divide!' In the middle of nowhere, dividing what? Top from bottom? East from West? Right from wrong?"

153

The train stopped. We got out to explore. A rustic wooden arch announced itself THE GREAT DIVIDE in important black letters. A small stream gurgled over black rock.

"Just as I thought," Mommie said. "Just a quaint western expression."

"No," I said. "It's the watershed. That little stream is going to end up a roaring river spilling into the Pacific. Up till now, rivers have been going north and east."

I'd learned that the year before so I could teach it.

The cherub was tugging at my skirt.

"Let's go eat," Mommie said. "You wouldn't mind joining us, would you? It's such a blessing for me that Ellen Ann likes you."

"Oh," I said. "Dinner."

I hadn't eaten since I had gotten on the train in Weyburn. I'd forgotten. I picked Ellen Ann up and followed Mommie through the train, past drummers reading newspapers as if there were nothing at all to look at, nothing at all out there to fear. As we entered the dining car, the train swayed and plunked me into a chair. I sat surrounded by sparkling white linen tablecloths, cut glass, gleaming silver.

"Do you mind Ellen Ann sitting beside you?" Mommie asked, positioning herself opposite me and taking out a cigarette. "It's so wearing."

I agreed.

"I've been trying to figure you out."

"What's to figure?"

"Your nationality. I thought you might be French or Italian."

"Wrong. Jewish."

"You're not serious."

"Yes, I am. Why? Are Italian and French women attractive?"

"No, not at all. Most of them are fat and greasy."

"Do you know any other Jews?"

"Heavens, no! We don't mix. You'll never find anyone like that living in our part of the city. Of course, when you're travelling, you meet all kinds of people you'd never dream of speaking to at home."

I saw red.

"You don't like much, do you? First it's black people, now it's the French, the Italians, and the Jews. You were probably

154

as sweet as your daughter once, too. If your lieutenant governor brother-in-law is as narrow-minded and stupid as you are, God help our country. I hope you noticed, by the way, I said 'our' country."

"No one has ever spoken to me that way!"

"It's about time they started."

She pulled Ellen Ann off the chair and stormed off. It's hard to storm anywhere in a moving train. The train lurched and she almost fell. I was sorry she hadn't. She had ruined the cut glass and the carnations and the white linen. She had ruined my appetite, too.

When the waiter arrived with a surly "Well?"—I'd only been waiting for half an hour, after all—I snapped, "Don't you start," and then I started to cry.

"Here, here," he said with alarm. "Don't cry. I'll lose my job if you cry."

I was lying in my berth almost asleep when I realized that the sun had disappeared with no sunset. Just gone. Dark. It wasn't any better in the morning, either. I pulled back the small curtain in my berth and looked out on grey mist curling around sombre pines and wet-black rock. A river boiled in the depths of a canyon far below. I got up.

"Where," I demanded of Ethelbert D. J. Bartholemew, "are the sunsets and sunrises?"

"Nae in the mountains, lass. The mountains cut them off. You need uninterrupted vistas for a proper sunrise."

"I'd kill myself if I had to live with day and night coming and going like you just pulled a window shade up or down."

"For a young lass out to see the world, you are in one mighty bad mood."

"Maybe I've seen enough of the world."

I told him about Mommie.

"Now look here, young lady, the glass is either half-empty or half-full. Same glass, all depends how you look at it. When you get back home, who you going to remember—that little thing who don't even have the sense to know what she's saying, or me who see to it you get where you going?"

"You," I said meekly.

"That's right," he said. "I could tell you stories about the black man in Canada that would curl your toenails. But you don't see me staying home and crying in my beer. Now you just get up and do what you gotta do."

Sometimes, he sounded definitely unScottish.

I went in for breakfast. Mommie was there. I smiled at her sweetly. Breakfast was delicious: freshly squeezed orange juice, Winnipeg goldeye and eggs, pancakes, and hot coffee. It made up for what I hadn't eaten the day before. It made up for Mommie.

We were escaping the mountains. The jagged peaks were receding, but the trees were taking over, Alice-in-Wonderland, Jack-in-the-Beanstalk trees. We could have driven the train right through some of those trees. Ethelbert D. J. Bartholemew couldn't understand what I was complaining about: the whole country—massive flat, massive sky, massive mountains, massive trees—was only various aspects of one thing. Massive.

It was over. We were in Vancouver, a city of large wooden houses dressed in green trees and soft skies. When Ethelbert D. J. Bartholemew helped me down to the platform, I didn't know how to thank him. Other people were giving him tips. "Nae from you, lass," he said. "I didna' do it for the money. If you should ever meet a young black lass or lad out in the world, just try to make their walk on this earth a little easier, as I have for you."

He was becoming more Scottish.

"Aye. This is the country for it. I'd nae be surprised if you are a Scot yourself in a day or two"—and he winked.

He handed my suitcase to the redcap with orders to get me safely to the train to Seattle, and turned to the other passengers, dusting coats and collecting tips.

Mommie was walking down the platform with her fur coat over one arm and Ellen Ann wriggling in the other. The lieutenant governor in full-dress uniform, an impressive and impressed-with-himself figure, awaited them. He reached for his niece. No doubt the lieutenant governor had never spoken to an Italian or a Jew, either.

I had three hours. I checked my suitcase. I went to look at the Pacific Ocean, mirror-blue with reflected clouds, sailboat clouds floating up to my feet. I sat down on a bench beside a dear little white-haired lady. She said ocean sunsets were the most beautiful in the world. She asked where I was from and commented on my accent. She was English. All her friends were English. In fact, everyone in Vancouver was English or Scottish. "It's such a comfort," she said. "I wouldn't be surprised if you are a Scot yourself, with your fine dark hair."

I said I wasn't, and reminded her that I had come from the prairies.

"No, dear," she said. "You are not an Indian, after all. Surely, your parents or your grandparents came from somewhere."

"They did. I do, too. The prairies. We're Canadian where I come from."

She patted my hand.

"Well, dear, you're young yet." She looked at me more closely. "You have to be careful, though, dear. There are all kinds of Japanese people here. With your thick eyebrows, you might be taken for a Japanese, and you wouldn't want that, would you?"

All I knew about Japan was what I had known at the beginning of the school year: geishas and cherry blossoms and buyers of scrap metal. What did she know that I didn't?

"Wouldn't I?" I asked.

"Oh, no! They're not like us, dear."

"Oh, I see," I said, and to my surprise, I laughed. And then I laughed because I could laugh, and I understood why Ethelbert D. J. Bartholemew told people—some people—that when he wasn't working on the train, he lived in a tree.

We watched the sunset together.

The ocean rose and fell with giant breaths rippling the muted rainbow hues of the Pacific sunset.

I got on the train. The porter—he was black—smiled as he showed me to my tiny berth. Ah, I thought to myself, another person with a cup half-full. I smiled. I was jostled off to sleep.

"I think she's dead, I declare, I think she's dead."

It was the porter. He had promised to wake me so I could see the sunrise, the most beautiful sunrise in all the world, the desert sunrise. I had missed it. I got up. From the observation car, there was rock and brown, rock and brown, rock and brown everywhere. But the sky was wide and wonderful, and the earth was solid under it, and the desert air was sweet.

Towards late afternoon, we were passing oil derricks, huge clanging metal stooks, and the air was no longer sweet. By the time we had chugged and whistled through miles and miles of little wooden pastel cottages to the Los Angeles train station, I was almost ill. I stood on the platform in a soup of nauseating, sulphurous heat amidst a swarm of people: a tall, ginger-haired man had my hand in his, a little round woman was kissing me, and four little freckled ginger-haired girls stared. Meyer was there, his honey-brown hair cut and combed to the side, not flopping into his eyes at all. He had the sweet shy smile I remembered the first time he had brought me roses. He shook my hand. My grandmother wasn't there. She was in an old folks' home.

I was led to a car, and we were on the highway, darting from lane to lane like water bugs on a slough. It was hours, it seemed, driving through rotten-egg heat and past drooping palm trees, before we stopped at one of the little cottages. A second ginger-haired man, thinner than the first, emerged with a sculptured woman at his side. We were ushered into a dry and bedraggled back yard to receive wedges of a lizard-skinned green fruit, watery and sweet with a ruby-red centre and black diamond seeds. I wanted to push those miles and miles of buildings away, to let the wind and sky flood in, to rub my face, my arms, my breasts with that ruby-red spring snow.

Suddenly, the air had cooled and sweetened and a curtain of night descended, and I knew that Uncle Manny was Mama's thin and jumpy youngest brother, and Uncle Paul was the one with kind eyes; Aunt Brenda was the round comfortable one, and Aunt Annette was the sculptured one. Uncle Paul had a fruit stand, and Uncle Manny was an MGM cameraman, and there were a million things to do in Los Angeles: shopping and symphonies, art galleries and beaches, night clubs . . . Everybody worked at MGM; Papa could have gotten a job at MGM instead of worrying about breaking land and branding cattle. What kind of life was it for their sister on a farm? I would see what life was like here: I could go back and talk sense into them.

Uncle Paul and Aunt Brenda and the four little girls were leaving. He had to be up at four to go to the central market. I asked the little girls if I could call them Annabelle and Clarabelle and Lulubell and Isabel. They giggled. I walked

Meyer to the car. He shook my hand again. It was hard to imagine that once he had called me Little Flower. I felt tired and sick and hot and sticky and disappointed. I took a bath. I filled the bathtub in the white tiled bathroom to the top and washed off mountains, cinders, and Mommie. I felt guilty: I was lying in enough water to bathe all six of us at home and then water the garden afterwards.

When I woke up the next morning, Uncle Manny had already gone to work. Aunt Annette was doing her nails and listening to the radio.

"Sssh," she said.

"They're in their favourite restaurant," a voice from the radio announced in boxing-match tones. "She's looking into her coffee cup, stirring it slowly. He's touching her wrist, folks, he's reaching for her hand. It looks as if they might be making up . . ."

"What's that about?" I asked.

"Ssssh. They've been fighting since yesterday. The reporters have been following them all night."

"Who?"

"Sssh."

I stuck my head out the door. The suffocating heat was building up.

I retreated.

"Why's Grandma in an old folks' home?" I asked.

"You don't expect me to take care of her, do you? She's paralyzed, and she's blind."

"But isn't this her house?"

She shrugged. Her nails were done. The doorbell rang.

"Oh, good! Francine and Laurel. You'll just love them. They can hardly wait to meet you. They want to know all about the Dionne Quintuplets."

Francine, Laurel, and Annette might have been triplets: manicured, marcelled, living examples of positive, comparative, and superlative adjectives. Blond, blonder, blondest. Blond, less blond, and least blond. They looked like they might be fun.

"Annette tells us you came to see your boyfriend," Francine, the less blond one said. "Honey, you're going to just love it here. I couldn't imagine living anywhere else. We've got just everything."

"Did you have to cross an ocean to get here?" Laurel, the least blond one asked. "It must be terrible to live in a place where there's snow all year."

"We're going to play gin rummy, Sara," Aunt Annette said. "Bring an ashtray, will you, honey? And take a cigarette yourself."

"I don't smoke."

"We'll soon fix that. Little Laurel didn't smoke, either, and now look at her."

I looked at her. Little Laurel, the least blond, was little, hard, and younger than me. She had been married three years, she said, and when she was first married, she was just like me: she didn't know anything. "For instance, sex," she said. "That's the hardest."

"I thought it was natural," I said.

"Oh, you know," she said. "What he likes and what you like."

"Never mind," Francine said. "She probably knows more than we do. You know what they say about country girls behind the barn."

"Hey," Annette said. "She's my niece."

"Not me," I said. "I don't know anything. Who's going to go out behind the barn in forty below weather? We don't even know how to play cards where I come from. We spend all our time knitting socks and skinning furs and praying for deliverance."

"Never mind," Francine comforted me. "It looks like your prayers have been answered. Annette says your boyfriend is really good-looking, and he plays the saxophone. I bet he's a lot of fun in the right places."

Laurel nodded.

"He's not my boyfriend," I said.

Three cokes each and two packages of cigarettes later, I had won ten dollars in quarters from them.

"Are you sure you never played before?" Annette asked.

"Green horn luck," I said.

"If you're too lucky, no one will want to play with you. We play every day, you know."

They knew more about the Dionne Quintuplets than I did.

I was awakened the next morning by the malodorous morning breeze. Annette and Uncle Manny got up at noon. Uncle Manny went out to a delicatessen for potato salad and cokes. I made coffee.

"How about some night life, kid?" Uncle Manny said. "We'll take you and your boyfriend out on the town."

"My boyfriend? I haven't heard from Meyer for three years. He could have been married by now, for all I knew."

"We'd know. The Saskatchewan Jews keep an eye on each other."

"How's Grandma?" I asked.

"I suppose," he said, "you want to go see her?"

"That's why I came."

"You might be sorry if you came all the way for that."

Uncle Manny drove me to the old folks' home—miles and miles away on the concrete river—and dropped me off. I was led to a room where eight old women lay in bed, old, old women with all the lines of time in their faces. My grandmother was one of them.

She traced the contours of my face and called me Eva. She said I could be Eva. But I wasn't. I was sorry that I wasn't. I read her Eva's letter, tried to be the link and description of years. And then I tried to put Eva's children together for her out of bits and pieces of people she knew: Saul with Papa's love of the land, me with Mama's temper, Leah with Papa's stubborn sense of justice, Ruth with Mama's love of story . . .

I tried to put my grandmother together for myself, but saw only an anxious, frightened old woman, afraid of her darkness, afraid of silence. She lay in a nursing home, perspiring in nauseating Los Angeles heat, in sheets that looked like they hadn't been changed for a month. Uncle Paul and Aunt Brenda had her father with them, Annette was busy with her sick mother, Uncle Manny didn't know from one day to the next if he would be called in to work—what could they do? Where else could she go? It had been a long life, a life over so quickly, and now each day was as long as a life.

Uncle Manny had come back to get me. She asked about her garden, the roses that used to give such pleasure. It was doing beautifully, he said, but it was hard to keep up, he said, with Annette nagging, uncertainty about work . . . I sat holding my grandmother's hand while he lied, and lied, and lied.

"Why is she in here?" I asked on the way out.

"Do you have any money?"

"What's that got to do with it?"

"This is a charity home. We can't afford anything better."

"Not even love. You can't afford even that. My grandfather died in our home, and it didn't cost us a cent."

I was driven directly to Aunt Brenda's and Uncle Paul's, a replica of my grandmother's cottage, spring-sky blue rather than faded pink, with a neat poinsettia hedge and magenta and yellow-gold bougainvillea winding around the windows. I would be staying there from now on, he said. The four Belles were delighted to see me.

"I think I've been evicted," I said.

"Oh," Aunt Brenda said comfortingly. "You've hurt your uncle's feelings. He'll get over it."

"I don't want him to get over it. They've got her house, and she's dying alone."

Uncle Paul was upset. Uncle Manny and Aunt Annette had lived with my grandmother and would inherit the house on the understanding that they would care for her. Uncle Paul and Aunt Brenda had taken in Aunt Brenda's father. He was feeding, clothing, and sheltering seven people in a tiny home—and forced to see his mother suffer.

"Come," Aunt Brenda said. "It's been a long day."

We piled into the car and puttered through the heat to the beach. The sun was just above the horizon, looking down onto the ocean and smiling back at itself, a warm golden glow in the arms of undulating silver-blue. Gilded sea lions basked on the rocks. The little ginger-haired girls wrapped themselves around their father's legs, and they went as a clump to play in the waves.

All that water, and at home it was being measured in teaspoons.

When Aunt Brenda asked what kept Mama and Papa on the farm, I thought about last summer's grasshoppers and relief feed for cattle, I thought about the dust that made little black ghosts out of my children. It would be a relief not to have to think of all that. Aunt Brenda and Uncle Paul had a sure business here. Maybe Mama and Papa were ready for a sure business.

Meyer was sitting on the verandah playing the saxophone for Aunt Brenda's father when we got back. He had brought my suitcase from Uncle Manny's.

"Ah trailed her," he said. "Ah followed her over the world. Ain't nothing goin' to keep me away from this woman. Throwed you out, eh? Ah'll pertect you. Ah'll pertect you from wolves and scoundrels and wicked aunts. And ah'll wait fer you, too, like ah bin waitin' on this here front stoop, jes' a settin' and a waitin'."

He sounded just like himself.

"Oh, Meyer," I said, and burst into tears.

"Hey there, Little Flower," he said, "you used to be as tough as that old prairie wool."

The four Belles stared in amazement. Aunt Brenda shooed them inside. "She's happy," she said. "Big people cry when they're happy."

"Are you happy?" Meyer demanded.

"I don't think so," I sniffed.

"Then stop it! You're setting a bad example."

"For who?"

"Me."

We went back to the beach. A delicate silver crescent floated above the shadowy palms, silver crescent glitters on liquid ebony waves. We waded into the water among the floating moons.

"What's wrong with you?" he asked again.

I didn't know.

"What happened today?"

I told him.

"Your grandmother could live with us."

"Yes," I sniffed.

"Does that mean you're going to marry me?"

"Maybe."

"Don't you love me?"

"Yes. I don't know. Do I?"

"If you loved me, you'd know."

163

"How do you know you love me?"

"Because I do. My body knows, and my mind knows. I miss you, and I smile about you when you're not here. You make me happy, and you make me mad. If you could swim, I'd drown you."

"I guess I love you," I said.

"You guess? You came all this way, crossed mountains and deserts, and you 'guess' you love me?"

I laughed.

"You don't believe me!" He waded out of the water and stomped up the beach.

"I was joking. I wasn't serious. Where's your sense of humour?"

He kept on walking.

"Meyer, I love you! I do! I love you, I love you, I love you!"

"Not good enough. Love by force is not good enough."

"I thought you'd be married," I screamed. "I didn't think you'd want me, I didn't think you cared. I can't say things like 'I love you.' I'm from the prairies, remember? My best friend is Norwegian."

"Will you marry me?" he shouted back.

"Yes."

"When?"

"Whenever you want."

He stomped back and held me.

When I got home, I sat up and talked to the moon. I would be safe with Meyer: he knew me, good tempered and bad tempered, irritating and adorable, smart as a whip and dumb as a doornail. He was comfortable. He was home. He was forever.

I awoke to a circle of four solemn little girls.

"Tell us a story. Mama said if we were quiet, you'd tell us a story."

I told them about the ugly duckling who grew up with no one to play with, no one to cuddle, just swimming all by herself on the water trough. By the end of the summer, she had become a large grey-and-white bird with a proud black head and a long, graceful neck. It was the dog who noticed her first. He stood on his hind legs and put his paws on the end of the trough, and barked in excitement for the other animals to come and see the beautiful bird. They came running—the cow who had chased her away because she couldn't moo, the chicken who had chased her away because she couldn't lay eggs—and saw a magnificent Canada Goose. The Canada Goose was so frightened that she flapped her wings—hard—and flew. They had frightened her into flying. She flew up, up, up into the sky, proud of her new wings, proud of herself.

They let me up.

Aunt Brenda had already left to help Uncle Paul. I made lunch for all of us, and four little girls and I trooped down to the fruit stand where my tall worried uncle and comfortable little aunt stood surrounded by a tiny mountain range of colour: green oranges, tawny grapefruit, lime limes, earth-brown pointed-hat figs . . . We walked home taking bits of the colour with us. By seven o'clock the curtain of night had fallen, and the palm trees rustled, not the soft-skirt rustle of poplars, but a crepe-paper streamer, taffeta-skirt rustle.

On the weekends, Meyer and I lived at the beach, saw the sun rise into a spindrift lemon ocean dawn, saw the sea gulls wheel against a water-pink evening sky. We wandered through gardens that were a spiny fantasy—tall, tree-like cactuses, low, fat cushion shapes—and came upon the original Blue Boy by Gainsborough in shimmering lake-water blue, hat in hand, about to step off the canvas and walk by our side. We went to a symphony under the stars and heard the caress of the evening breeze in the notes of the violin, heard the clarity of the prairie stars in the notes of the piano.

And then there were only a few weeks left.

"*Nu?*" my grandmother said. The little girls and I had arrived for our twice-weekly visit with fresh fruit, fresh flowers, and fresh sheets. "When will I meet him? You talk about the apartments you look at, you tell me how wonderful he is, but you don't bring him to meet your grandmother. What kind of business? In a few weeks, you will go back to teach. Who knows if I will be alive when you get back?"

I promised to bring him.

Aunt Annette was at Uncle Paul's and Aunt Brenda's sitting

at the kitchen table in a white linen suit, white hat, and white gloves: the superlative of blond.

"Honey," she said, "your uncle feels just terrible, and it's all my fault. We want to make it up to you."

"What about making it up to my grandmother?"

"Grandma understands, don't you worry about that. She doesn't want you going back to your mother with any misunderstandings, either."

"It sounds like I don't have any choice," I said.

"No, I guess you don't, honey, and neither do I. Your uncle wants me to take you shopping and buy you some real chic clothes so we can take you and your boyfriend out on the town. We wouldn't want your mother and father saying we didn't give you a good time."

She left me her manicure set and made me promise to teach all my friends up in Canada how to use it before I came back the following summer.

That evening, I informed Meyer that he and I would be seeing The Life. It would be a moonlit night, I said; I would lean languidly against a palm tree and raise yearning eyes; he would draw me to him manfully, and I would melt into his arms.

It wasn't moonlit. We waited outside a warehouse in a night that was dark, humid, and still. A heavy wooden door slid open. A thug peeked through. We filed in, Annette first in slinky scarlet, me in mysterious indigo, Meyer and Uncle Manny in baronial white. Four whiskeys—smooth, Canadian contraband whiskey—appeared on the bar. Uncle Manny and Aunt Annette disappeared into a haze of smoke. Meyer and I settled ourselves on stools. A woman in a shapeless powder-grey dress was pacing between two bookies—"Come on, Turtle!"—and placing one-hundred-dollar bets—"Come on, Dancer!": with neither smile nor frown, she was losing every time.

"Stop it," Meyer snarled. "You're smiling."

"I am not," I snarled back.

Uncle Manny had returned. A blond city-slicker at his side took my hand firmly in his. "In Los Angeles," he said, gazing intently into my eyes, "women don't stay married long."

"Come on," Meyer said. "This is enough Life."

"Hey!" I said.

We were out the door.

"When will I get a chance to do anything like this again?"

"Never."

"Now what? It's early, and I'm all dressed up."

"We'll go to the beach for our romantic walk in the moonlight so you can gaze up at me with yearning eyes, that's what."

"There is no moon."

"So what? You love the beach, remember? Lapping waves, soft ocean beaches . . ."

"That's Nature. This is Life."

"This isn't Life. This is Death."

We drove to the beach. The tide was out.

"We'll come here every evening," Meyer said. "We'll bring our children."

"Am I crazy?" I asked. "What is that awful rotten-egg smell all day?"

"I talk children, and she talks rotten eggs."

"Nobody ever mentions it. Am I the only one who smells it?"

"Sulphur from the Bakersfield oil fields," he said. "It comes in with the land breeze during the day. You get used to it."

"Are you used to it?"

"The nights," he continued, "such soft, moonlit nights. Soft moonlit nights all year round. No blizzards. No winter coats. No boots. No foot-warmers or horsehair blankets."

"Meyer, what did you think of that 'million-dollar boat' we took to Catalina Island?"

"What about it?"

"It was a tub. A rickety wooden tub with a wooden cage in the centre for a bathroom. I saw one of the Princess ships that ferries between Vancouver and Victoria. It was a work of art compared to that, a real ship, with upper and lower decks and restaurants and polished brass, everything luxury boats are supposed to have. But we don't advertise a 'million-dollar boat.' And the May Company. Everybody calls it the 'biggest store in the world.' Who cares if Jack Benny met Mary Livingstone there? It's two floors of poorer quality than we have in Estevan, let alone Regina. And not as big as the department store in Regina, either. If the May Company is the biggest store in the world, then R. H. Williams must be the biggest in the universe. Annette and her MGM wives say they wouldn't live anywhere else. Obviously, they've never been anywhere else. Are you glad you moved here?"

"I wrote a song about it," he said. "It's called, 'Imagine the Pleasure of Not Worrying about the Weather.' Down here, people like it when there's no rain. I go off to work every day knowing that no matter how bad things are, I'll still sell insurance. In fact, the worse things are, the more I sell. I got what I wanted, Little Flower—I don't have to depend on the sky for my living."

"Are you happy?" I asked.

"Yes'm," he said. "Yes, ma'am, I am. Like they say, the only thing missing from my life is a good woman."

I took him to meet my grandmother.

"Finally," she said. She took his hand, held it, and pronounced him a good man. "So why did you wait so long, Sara?"

I couldn't remember why.

Meyer glared at me over the bed.

"She can't remember? Because I wasn't enough for her. She wasted three years of our married life because she thought she wanted to stay on the farm."

"It wasn't wasted. You got settled here, and I got my teacher training."

"You won't need to teach."

"Don't be silly. We can use the money. Besides, you don't think I want to stay home and play gin rummy with the MGM wives all day, do you?"

"Needing the money has nothing to do with it. You'll never get a teaching job here."

"Why not? Don't they hire married women?"

"They don't hire anybody who doesn't have a university degree."

"You're kidding."

"No, I'm not."

"Why didn't you say anything before?"

He was silent.

"I can't live like that. All anyone ever talks about here is which movie star is divorcing which. The only thing they know about Canada is the Dionne Quintuplets and the North-West Mounted Police. They don't even talk about the depression in this country, let alone doing something about the palm trees that are dying because the city can't afford to water them. If every house watered one tree . . . But no. They sit and play gin rummy and smoke all day."

"Now, Sara, be fair," Grandma said. "That's Annette and her friends. Brenda isn't like that."

"What about me?" Meyer said. "For God's sake, what about me?"

"You like insurance, you like the beach—you'll have everything you want. I'll have only you. I'll drive you crazy. It's true, Meyer. You know it's true."

I waited for a response. I reached for his hand. He pulled away. I tried to explain what I now knew about my grandfather, about my mother and father, about myself.

"Everyone feels sorry for Mama and Papa because it's hard for them on the prairie. But it's no harder than what Uncle Paul is doing, and it's exciting. They've been part of something growing—our farm, Short Haul . . . They couldn't have done that here. And I won't be able to, either."

"What about your grandmother? We promised her she could live with us."

"An old woman who will die tomorrow is not a reason," Grandma announced firmly. "She has given me a summer I never thought possible. What more gift can I ask of a young girl?"

We left, drove home through the sticky-soup heat. He shook my hand and called me Sara. The little girls gathered. "Are you still happy?"

"No," I said.

"Why not?"

"Because I'm not like the other chickens," I said, "and I'm not sure I'm a Canada Goose, either."

That night, sitting on the front step in the night cool, Meyer's song kept going through my head—"Imagine the Pleasure of Not Worrying about the Weather." I would never laugh with him again. My grandmother would lie through long sticky days, days that crawled like flies over dirty plates, and I was going back to clear-note stars and blue-shadow snows, to inquisitive children and not enough books. I was going back to Mama's disapproval. I was going back to a future alone.

I was terrified.

I was standing on the Weyburn platform, and I had made my announcement.

"You're a foolish girl," Mama said abruptly, turning back to the car.

"Never mind her," Papa said. "I never liked him. He always walked around the yard as if he was afraid of getting his feet wet."

But I did mind her.

"It's not Meyer," I said. "You don't know what it's like. The Philippinos stick to the Philippinos, and the Jews to the Jews, and the Armenians to the Armenians—it's like living on one of Aunt Sophie's shelves. If you're a bottle of bay rum, you don't mix with the vanilla, and you don't move in case the chewing tobacco wants to take your spot."

The twins laughed. Saul hugged me.

"No, really," I said. "We would never even have met the Dahls because they're Norwegian; Papa would never have been friends with Dr. Lowe because he's a doctor . . ."

"How's my mother?" Mama asked.

She was fine, I lied. She was living with Uncle Manny and Aunt Annette, and she was fine. And Los Angeles didn't have rotten-egg air, and nobody thought we lived in tepees.

We drove from Weyburn through dry land. It had been a good year, almost no crop, but no dust storms, either. We drove home with our heads up in the sky.

The twins and Saul and I were up till midnight. They wanted to hear everything. I told them everything. "Gee," Ruth said, "gambling! Didn't anyone shoot you?"

"A real painting," Leah sighed. "Imagine a real painting and not a picture of one. I bet it's like talking to live people instead of talking to them on the telephone."

Saul said he was glad I was back—a family wasn't the same without its parts—but he hoped I wouldn't be sorry.

When I walked into the schoolyard the next morning, the children stopped and stared as if I were an apparition.

"What's the matter?" I asked.

"Gunnar said you'd never come back. His Ma said nobody in their right mind would come back if they didn't have to."

"Oh," I said.

Mr. Gallagher was standing at the top of the steps.

"Welcome back," he said.

"What? Oh. I live here. You don't have to welcome me back."

"You should have a better year this year."

"I should? Why?"

"The twins are gone."

"Ray and Roy?"

"They're in the Weyburn Asylum."

"But they aren't crazy. They just can't sit still. We'll never see them again. When people go in there, they never come out. How could you let them send two little nine-year-olds in with all those grown-up crazy people?"

"Whoa! Hold your horses. I didn't do it. Their parents did. They couldn't handle them. How was your trip?"

All of a sudden, I remembered who we were, and who he wasn't. He wasn't Meyer. I didn't like him.

"Wonderful," I said. "Absolutely wonderful. A veritable garden of delights."

And it had been.

I was presented with new students by proud brothers and sisters. Two presented themselves—David, a tiny matchstick child who sat watchful, pale, alone, and Donny, a sturdy little boy with Beth's triangle face and wide grey eyes. Beth was back on the farm, still lovely and a fierce mother, with an equally sturdy Swede who adored her. David was in grade one, Donny in grade two. I stationed Amy, all blue-eyed, blond-plaited motherly concern, between them.

The children knew all about the disappearance of the twins, but it had happened weeks ago, and wasn't nearly as interesting as picture-postcards of water that was a vast plain of reflected sky, of cactuses that were trees, and fish that flew . . .

"Who'd want to go to a place where the sun disappears

without any colours?" Gunnar asked. It was recess, and he had come back to show off.

"Are mountains as high as elevators?" Amy asked. They looked at me and waited for an answer. I knew they would never believe it.

"Mountains," I said, "are as high as clouds."

They didn't believe it.

That evening, sitting in the silence and warmth of a room children have been in, mist-locked mountains and silent pines, gilded sea lions and elusive tides, Ethelbert D. J. Bartholemew and Mommie . . . might never have been.

I walked home through the pasture. September's brown-eyed susans and coneflowers bowed gently to the bees.

"Tsippa is engaged," Mama accused as I walked in the door.

"That's a relief," I said.

"Don't be smart," she said. "I wish you were more like her. You don't have to be in love to get married, you know. A good provider is just as important."

"I don't need to be provided for. Women teachers who aren't married get the same salary as men. Besides, that's not why I didn't marry Meyer. I do love him. I love him very much."

She didn't understand.

Each morning, a matchstick child walked out of the west along railroad tracks that were filaments of morning light under an early sun. While Donny threw himself at the world and got himself into trouble, David sat watching. Outside of the classroom on our field trips, he was like one of the foxes or pheasants—quick, elusive, comfortable with nooks and crannies. When we went to see the Dahl's pet fox, the young pup sat on Mr. Dahl's knee with his pointed ears and bright black eyes, and looked straight at David. The next day, David drew a curious little fox with pointed black ears looking down on a tiny train that was only half an inch long on the page, but had enough presence to fill the room. I taught him to count with box cars and foxes.

"What's wrong with you?" Ruth asked one morning. "Get out on the wrong side of bed?"

"No," I said. "I can't teach simple addition. I couldn't teach it all night."

"Why don't you take them to Aunt Sophie's store?" Mama said. "If you buy two penny candies, that's addition. How do you think I taught you?"

"I thought my teachers taught me."

"Don't be silly," she said. "Your teachers didn't know anything about teaching."

"Gee," the children said when I talked to them later that morning. "Is that all adding is?"

"Sure," I said, as if I'd known it all the time. "But maybe we should have our own store first to practise."

In no time at all, we had stocks of oatmeal, baking powder, sugar (all empty boxes and cans and sacks, of course), and everything else that could be needed by man, woman, or child right there in the Eaton's catalogue, all ready to be paid for, cut out, and delivered. We had a shoe-box cash register and match-box drawers filled with paper cutout money and big and little button coins. We were storekeepers and clerks who had to be able to read and write the items we stocked; we were customers who had to be able to add up our purchases, to subtract to be sure we had enough. (We always had enough; we never had to charge it.) The day David, the littlest grade one, made his order for crayons so he could teach his baby sister to draw trains, we were all proud.

I walked home with David that afternoon to tell his mother that now when he watched, he also listened.

It was a three-mile walk along the railroad, David's favourite thing in all the world, pencil lines across the land, lines of steel that went forever and ever and ever, until they just disappeared into the sky. A crow sat on a rock and cawed at us. Gophers sat up and flicked their tails. Canada Geese called to us from the height of their perfect V. He showed me his secret, two perfect speckled Killdeer eggs in a feathered saucer of earth. They didn't have a mother.

As we approached a grey and weathered farm—a small barn, a chicken coop, a granary, an outhouse, and a two-room shack set on the slope of a hill—he slipped away.

The kitchen door was open. His mother was standing at the stove, stirring a pot with one hand, holding a *True*

Confessions magazine with the other, and rocking a baby with her foot. Lazy flies crawled over dirty plates. Chickens pecked at clothes on the floor. A dog opened an eye and raised an ear.

"Mrs. . . ." I began.

Her head snapped up.

"You! What are you doing here? Spying!"

"I came to tell you that your son . . ."

"Son?" she hissed, cutting me off. "I don't have a son! I have a daughter!" She indicated the cradle with her foot. "Did I know he had a son when I married him? What has that little sneak been telling you?" She brandished her wooden spoon at me and advanced.

"Don't be ridiculous," I said. "He's a sweet little boy. I just came to tell you how well he's doing."

"Do you visit every farm? Get out! Get out of here! And don't think that little sneak won't hear about it!"

I left.

I was in school early, watching for a small figure walking out of the sky. In the middle of the morning, I looked up and saw him standing at the bottom of the hill. When he came in, he sat surrounded by walls, desks, children—and as distant as the moon.

I had a dream of a matchstick child playing alone on alabaster hills under an indigo sky. I woke up in a panic.

We were ready to go to Aunt Sophie's, each of us with a real order and two schoolboard pennies tied into our handkerchiefs so they wouldn't jump out. We trooped across the frosted fall grasses and marched with important steps along the wooden sidewalk. Aunt Sophie, seated by the counter, welcomed us gravely as we entered the store. We scattered among the counters and kegs and barrels with their bolts of cloth and boxes of bloomers, treasures of nails and rounds of cheese.

Suddenly, David stood stock still as a voluminous black shawl swirled out of the spaces, and he was enveloped in the folds of black that were his stepmother. "My son!" she said. "My punishment from God." She stood back from the stiff child and left him, like a dead thing, among the shelves.

Aunt Sophie was filling orders with great ceremony and

giving change for real money when she suddenly darted out from behind the counter. She was running for David's mother, and she had her broom in her hand.

"For months!" she screamed, swatting at her with her broom. "I've been watching you! It's bad enough no one can pay their bills, you have to steal, too? In front of children? What kind of business!"

Aunt Sophie swatted her right out of the store as cans tumbled out from under the black shawl. When I looked for David, he was gone. The children's laughter was quelled only by Aunt Sophie's dark mutterings.

"How would you feel if it was your mother?" I asked on the way back to the school.

They giggled and snickered the rest of the day, and the day after that. For the next week, I spent too much time watching for a tiny figure walking out of the sky.

"Miss Schiller," he began in a business-like manner. It was Mr. Gallagher, the first time he had come into my classroom all year. "What's wrong with you?"

I shrugged. He glared. I was delighted.

"I spoke as your principal," he said tightly. "I have come to discuss a school project."

"Shoot," I said. "I'm your man."

"A midwinter celebration," he spat at me. "The community coming together in song and story and dance to celebrate the winter solstice."

"You mean a Christmas concert," I said. "The Jewish parents don't mind, as long as there's no crêche or Jesus in it."

"The Jews, Miss Schiller, are not the problem."

"Glad to hear it," I said. "So?"

"The celebration of the winter solstice is a tradition begun long before Christianity," he continued. "I'm sick of my Lutheran and Anglican and Baptist and Catholic and God-knows-what-all parents telling me how I should be doing things in my school. We enjoy a separation of church and state in this country, and I intend to take advantage of it."

"Right, sir, anything you say. Song and story and dance. Community coming together."

"Thank you, Miss Schiller."

He glanced at my sunset as he left the room. It was brilliant.

I had no idea where I was going to get song and story and dance. I worried about it all night, and I worried about it with the children the next day. The children weren't worried at all— that was easier than losing your hat in the wind: Amy's mother sang Scottish songs, Donny's mother Beth told ghost stories that would scare the tail off a coyote, Chaim and Moishe and Yisroel's father played the fiddle . . .

But what would we give in return? We could sing some of the songs that we had learned, but what else? Science experiments? Art? Pressed flowers? Vegetables?

Vegetables. We would tell them about vegetables. The students would work in pairs to do research on the vegetable of their choice.

Amy and David chose the cucumber growing in secret under fuzzed diamond-shaped leaves, a surprise born of small yellow flowers. They found out that cucumbers were always one or two degrees cooler than the air around them, and that was where the expression "cool as a cucumber" came from. They found out that ladies sliced cucumbers and put them on their faces. They found out that pickles were a way to eat cucumbers all year round. They found out that you could make a cucumber costume out of green crepe paper, and when you were inside it, nobody could see you.

They found out that they were friends.

I got used to seeing Amy and David walk to the railroad track each afternoon and part ways, David to walk into evening, Amy to walk to the dawn.

One morning, David didn't come into the classroom when the bell was rung. I found him huddled in the corner beside the school steps. I knelt down, held a small tear-stained face in my hands. There was the loneliness of the ages in a small boy's eyes.

He couldn't come. He couldn't come to the midwinter celebration and be a cucumber.

I wiped his tears. I would think of something, I said: I promised him I would think of something.

He came inside and took his seat. Amy talked about trains and foxes until he smiled.

I thought of talking to David's father. But I couldn't go back to the farm. I would have to wait until he came to the store. I asked Aunt Sophie to call me. David's father, a tall, lean man, looked me in the eye only once to tell me it was none of my affair.

I thought of a dress rehearsal. You were supposed to have a practice before the real concert, I explained to the students, in costume and just the way you would do it for real to make sure everything was all right. Big people did that. We would do that. We would have a concert for ourselves. We would have refreshments, and we would be the audience, sitting in front to see the parts we weren't in, instead of lining up in the cloakroom waiting our turn.

We diagrammed the magic of science and colour, we cut and pinned and practised. Finally, we trooped across to the community hall to set up the benches and sweep the stage. Oranges and apples from Aunt Sophie and milk and cookies and sandwiches from our mothers awaited us. We were ready for an afternoon of song and story.

Donny told his ghost story; the memory fashion show of skirts and parasols and spats and high-button blouses swept across the stage; the vegetables quarrelled about who was most important in the garden. Mr. and Mrs. Cucumber—with cool-as-a-cucumber voices—settled it: what good was Miss Carrot's vitamin A if Mrs. Farmer died of scurvy without Mr. Tomato's vitamin C? We laughed and clapped and cheered. When the whole school got up on stage to sing "Winter Wonderland," we were so proud of ourselves that we sang it again.

There was pride and the light of laughter in the eyes of the tiny boy who ran off clutching a green crepe-paper costume, a tiny boy caught between silver hills and pewter skies.

It was just as we had dreamed it.

There was a new moon that clear December night, a pearl crescent with enough of a hook to hold a pail of water. The world was luminous.

We were lining up with butterflies in our stomachs when Amy disappeared. I found her in tears in the cloakroom.

"Donny says I'm boney and ugly and my shoes have holes in them, and I should have stayed home like David did."

"That's not why David didn't come," I said.

"Yes, it is," she sniffled.

"Are you sure?"

She nodded.

"Oh, Amy," I said.

"Don't cry, Miss Schiller," she said.

I sat down on the cloakroom floor beside her. She looked at my shoes. The soles were wearing through. Amy was delighted. She had thought that only little people got holes in the soles of their shoes. Donny, we decided, had holes in his shoes, too, and that was why he was making us feel bad.

The vegetables had sung their happy garden song, the senior room had enacted a Norse legend; I was just striking the chords for their Major Bowes Amateur Hour when I saw Papa and Uncle Yacov run out of the room. Suddenly, the whole hall was on its feet.

It was the orange silk again, the orange silk dancing and fluttering in the distance, dancing and fluttering against the crystal-star night. A cluster of sleighs and cutters, drawn by the silk, unwound onto the night velvet road. I stood in the silence of the darkened room and watched the chain thread its way to our farm as the flames reached the moon. I walked home, mesmerized by the flames. My father stood in front of his burning barn, silhouetted by tatters of silk flames. His eyes held crystal tears with gold fire centres.

Little feet were stamping snow off their boots in the cloakroom.

"My Ma says your Pa should be horsewhipped."

It was Donny.

I dashed into the cloakroom. David stood, trapped, in a circle of children nodding accord.

"What's this about horsewhipping?" I demanded.

"My mother says," Amy explained, "anybody who burns down a barn should be burned along with it."

"Who said anything about the barn being burned?"

"Everybody knows David's father did it. Constable Yeaman wants your father to press charges."

"How do you know that?"

"Everybody knows that."

"No, they don't."

"Yes, they do. His father's hands are burned. Gunnar's Pa said."

"If my father believed someone had burned down his barn, he would press charges. He's the justice of the peace, after all. Justice is more important to a justice of the peace than to anyone else, isn't it?"

"You're going to make us say we're sorry, aren't you," Amy said.

"Yes," I said. "Because you are."

"Donny never said he was sorry to me," she said.

I turned to Donny, to the wide eyes of his mother. He looked at his shoes.

"He would feel better if he did. And you'll both feel better if you say it to David."

"In front of everybody?"

"You said it in front of everybody."

"Aw, shucks," Amy said.

But David was gone. I ran after him, caught him, held him as he wept the heartache of all the prairie.

I sat that afternoon in the silence of a room children have been in and fought my own tears.

The winter holiday was haunted by the fire. From the kitchen window, from the living-room window, we saw charred timber. Papa stood for long hours, simply stood, staring into the void that had been the barn. Mama was desperate. She had never seen him like this: through drought, depression, lawsuits, he had never been like this. He had been defeated, he had finally been defeated.

School started on one of those clear January days when smoke from the chimney is a white ladder to heaven against an endless depth of sky. The children were sharp bits of life against the snow hills. Except for David, who sat no longer guarded, only distant, they had forgotten the fire.

All that week I tried to get a response from David, but it was the argument about oceans and mountains that finally did it. Moishe and Chaim and Yisroel knew all about oceans. They had crossed the ocean to come to Canada. Oceans were like prairie: oceans, they said, left as much room for the sky as the prairie. Donny scoffed. Mountains were the best, he said. He bet you could see clear to North Dakota from a mountain. Oh, no, Amy said. If you stood on a mountain, nobody could see you, not even the sky, not like here where as soon as you stood up, the whole world was different.

"I like it when nobody can see me," a small voice said.

It was David.

"You just have to run away if you don't want anyone to see you," Donny said. "When I get big, I'm taking off. I might not even wait."

I walked half-way home with David along the railroad tracks that evening. A tiny boy disappeared into the violet snow shadows, a tiny boy balancing on a pencil line of his imagination. I crossed the pasture, added my tracks to the printed conversation in the snow—partridge and fox, rabbit and coyote, field mouse and deer.

Mama was waiting for me.

"Tsippa wrote to Aunt Sophie. They are inviting you to Winnipeg."

"What for? So you can marry me off, too?"

Suddenly, her eyes were blue pools of tears.

"I don't know what to do, Sara. I don't know what to do for Aaron—how am I supposed to know what to do for you?"

"Mama," I said. "You're not supposed to."

I dreamed about David that night. He was balancing on a pencil line of steel, walking into the deepening sky, walking, walking, walking. I saw him curl into a snowdrift and snuggle into sleep. I tried to wake him. In my dream, I tried to wake him.

I woke up in a panic.

And ran to the telephone to ring the emergency number. David's asleep, I said, he's asleep in the snow on the railroad track going west.

One of the Wilkinson boys found him, found a small boy curled into sleep in the snow. The Wilkinsons kept him for a week, massaging him, soothing him, while he lay small and bewildered against a pillow.

At school there was an empty desk no one would sit in, and enormous half-inch trains no one would take down. We were waiting for David to come back. Donny cried, and Amy wanted to know if it was her fault. I could only say that we were all snowflakes, one as important as the other, glittering and shining with our own six-pointed beauty for a time, that life had a beginning, a middle, and an end, with good and bad in it that we didn't always understand. We happened, life happened, life happened to us: sometimes we were lucky, and we happened to life.

They nodded wisely.

"Like when Mr. Dahl found the baby fox beside its dead mother and saved it," they said.

"Yes," I said.

That evening, I walked along the railroad tracks, the pencil lines David loved to draw across a snowy page. The class was sending him our crayons.

His eyes lit up when he saw me, widened with amazement when he saw his gift. We sat together while he told me what he would draw when he got big: the bigger you got, he said, the bigger you could draw. He would draw a picture for Amy and Donny and Chaim and Hans . . .

His father came in then, ashamed when he saw me, embarrassed in front of his son. David slipped his hand into mine. I got up to leave. David's hand tightened.

"Do you believe in dreams?" I asked his father. "I had a dream—" I began, and told them of the dream of David in the snow.

"Your son is mine," I said. "A dream has made him mine."

He looked away, nodded, crumpled his cap in his hand. "Maybe it's for the best," he said. "The best for David. My wife . . . The lantern just slipped you know." And he was gone.

"What do you think, David?" I asked. "Do you want to live with me?"

He shrugged. I hugged him.

I called Saul, and he came to get us. We drove home in the cutter over blue-shadow snows, warm together under the horsehide blanket. Mama was waiting with open arms. "Ah," she said, "my first grandchild." Papa looked askance.

During the day, Mama sat David in a chair and chattered to him while she worked and he drew pictures—Mama washing clothes, Mama sitting on a train. In the afternoons, the twins fought over him. He became a laughing, cherished child.

181

In March, David took his first steps. I carried him out to Papa, and tried not to see the snow-covered timbers. We stood, walked for Papa. Papa picked him up and hugged him, a small dark head against silver white, shy delight against emptiness and pain.

"I told you that he said he didn't mean it, Papa," I said. "The lantern slipped."

"Don't be a fool," he said. "What was he doing in my barn in the first place? When have any of us refused to help out? I've been losing things for months—did he have to steal? And what good is 'didn't mean it' now? I'm an old man. How many times can I start over?"

"You're letting one man destroy you. You're the one who always said, 'Wait, and you'll see what their children will become.'"

"I'm not a saint," he said.

"He's just one man, Papa."

"Yes," he said, "and I'm just one man."

Mr. Dahl came riding up behind us.

"By yumpin'," Mr. Dahl said, throwing his hat on the snow, "Aaron Schiller is feeling sorry for Aaron Schiller long enough."

"Oh, I see," Papa said tiredly, "my daughter thinks I'm a saint, and you think I'm God. I can't afford a chicken coop right now. What am I supposed to do, build a barn out of thin air?"

"This whole country was built out of thin air. And, by yumpin', the air is not so thin now as 1905 when we had only two hands and a cow and not two words the same between us."

"What about hope?" I said. "You had that, whether you knew the word or not."

Papa's jaw tightened. There was a flash of black anger behind the brown-gold eyes. Thor laughed.

"Good. When Aaron is mad, we get things done."

David and I left them talking about getting things done.

Mr. Gallagher was standing meekly at the door.

"I want you to know I'm sorry about everything," he said.

"Are you?"

"Yes, I are."

"What for? You didn't burn down the barn."

"Listen, Miss Schiller," he snapped back, "I mean it."

A birdcage was plunked down on my desk. A canary fluttered and chirped, a tiny bit of summer sunshine with charcoal-tipped wings.

"You're not going to cry, are you?" he said. "I thought Dickie would cheer everybody up. I thought you and David needed it. He always cheers me up. I'm sorry about the barn. What's a farm without a barn? I know everybody's on relief, but you'll see—there'll be another barn."

"Mr. Gallagher . . ."

"Call me Sean. Even if you don't like me, call me Sean."

"Are you really apologizing? Even for being such an underhanded rat last year?"

"Yes."

And then I did cry. I cried for David, for Papa, for Meyer, for the prairie, for myself.

"Oh, Sara," Sean said.

We could still be friends, Sean said, we could only be friends, we should only be friends.

He wiped my tears with his handkerchief. I thanked him. Thank you, Sean, I said.

He drove me and the summer-sunshine bird home.

The canary sang and sang and sang—sang us right into spring.